WHERE THE
BROKEN HEART
STILL BEATS

CYNTHIA ANN PARKER

Center for American History
The University of Texas at Austin

CAROLYN MEYER

WHERE THE BROKEN HEART STILL BEATS

THE STORY OF CYNTHIA ANN PARKER

GULLIVER BOOKS

HARCOURT BRACE JOVANOVICH, PUBLISHERS

San Diego   New York   London

HBJ

Library of Congress Cataloging-in-Publication Data
Meyer, Carolyn.
Where the broken heart still beats/by Carolyn Meyer.—1st ed.
p.   cm.
Summary: Having been taken as a child and raised by Comanche
Indians, thirty-four-year-old Cynthia Ann Parker is forcibly returned
to her white relatives, where she longs for her Indian life and her
only friend is her twelve-year-old cousin Lucy.
ISBN 0-15-200639-7(hc).   0-15-295602-6(pbk.)
1. Comanche Indians—Captivities—Juvenile fiction. [1. Parker,
Cynthia Ann, 1827?–1864—Juvenile fiction. 2. Parker, Cynthia
Ann, 1827?–1864—Fiction. 3. Comanche Indians—Captivities—Fiction.
4. Indians of North America—Captivities—Fiction. 5. Frontier and
pioneer life—Fiction.]   I. Title.
PZ7.M5685Wh   1992
[Fic]—dc20   92-2578

Designed by Lisa Peters
Printed in the United States of America
First edition
A B C D E   A B C D E (pbk.)

For

ALAN AND AMANDA

TEXAS C. MID-NINETEENTH CENTURY

Part I

NADUAH

CHAPTER ONE

From Lucy Parker's journal, January 24, 1861

Our strange cousin arrived yesterday. I cannot believe this woman is our kin, although Grandfather, who brought her and her little girl from Fort Cooper, swears it is so. Her skin is darkened by the sun, and she seems as wild as the Indians she has lived with since a child, although Mrs. Evans, the captain's wife, did her best to clean her up and dress her in civilized clothing. At times she babbles in her strange tongue, but mostly she keeps silent, clutching the baby girl and staring at us like a cornered animal. Her eyes are as blue as my own, but I confess her look frightens me.

She speaks almost no English and seems to understand little, save her own name: Cynthia Ann. Grandfather says that when he first saw her ten days ago, he was not sure this shy, wild creature really was his long-lost niece, kidnapped by Comanches twenty-five years ago. Yet when he spoke her name she responded.

"She laid her hand upon her breast," he told us, his own voice trembling with feeling, "and said, 'Me—Cynthia Ann.' That was all."

Now she and her child are to live here with us. The little girl, called Topsannah, looks entirely Indian, as though not a drop of white blood flows in her veins. Everyone in the family seems happy to have them here, and there is much rejoicing and thanking God for her return to us after all those years as a prisoner of the murderous redskins. But if our cousin is at all grateful, she does not show it.

"Poor thing, poor thing," my mother and sister Martha say. "Small wonder, after all she's suffered." But I am sure they have no idea what to do with her now that she is here.

I know her story, of course, having heard it from as far back as I can remember. It began when our people—the Parker family—came to Texas from Illinois in the 1830s in covered wagons pulled by teams of oxen. My great-grandfather, Elder John Parker, three of his sons, and grandsons along with their wives and children settled by the Navasota River where they built a fort of log cabins and blockhouses, surrounded by a stockade to protect them from the marauding Indians. The family had been farming there for two years when the Comanches raided Parker's Fort, killed several people, and took captive two women and three children.

Cynthia Ann Parker and her younger brother John were among the captives. Her father was killed, but her mother managed to escape with two younger children. That was on May 19, 1836, twelve years before I was born. Cynthia Ann was nine years old when she was kidnapped, the same age our Sarah is now. When I look at my young sister, I can imagine the terror little Cynthia Ann must have felt as the bloodthirsty savages carried her off.

Our family has never forgotten this horror. Grandfather, her uncle, has tried unceasingly for twenty-five years to find her and bring her back. He worked especially hard after his wife and seven of their children died—all but my father, Isaac, his namesake—carried off by fevers and tragic accidents.

A few years after Cynthia Ann's capture, when she was about twelve—my age—white traders saw her in an Indian camp and offered a ransom for her. But the Indians would not let her go. Several years passed, and Grandfather learned that she was married to a Comanche warrior and had children. I shudder to think what her life with them was like.

He had nearly given up hope of saving her, but two weeks ago something unbelievable happened. A group of our Texas Rangers, including my sister Martha's sweetheart, Jedediah, attacked a Comanche camp up by the Pease River. Those Comanches have raided settlements throughout this area, killing and scalping and looting, and Capt. Sul Ross, Jedediah's friend and the leader of the group, determined to put a stop to their activities and teach them a lesson. After the battle in which many Indians were killed, the Rangers discovered Cynthia Ann and took her and the baby to Fort Cooper, where she was cared for until Grandfather arrived. But this woman who Grandfather insists is his brother's daughter does not have the look of one who has been rescued. She looks like one who is imprisoned.

Grandfather's friend, Mr. Mason, a trader who understands the Comanche tongue, traveled with him to Fort Cooper and has since come here to visit, but even he cannot get her to say much. She only asks repeatedly for her husband and two sons.

Grandfather says she has been treated cruelly for so long that it will take much kindness and patience to bring her truly back to us. Yesterday he spoke to me privately. He knows that I learned my letters in school well enough to read our family Bible. (He does not know that I keep this journal. It is my private book, and I make sure that it is well hidden from the others, among the patches I am saving for a quilt.)

"You stay with her, Lucy," Grandfather said. "You help her to find her English again. Maybe that way she will find her soul, as well."

But I fear that will be like trying to teach a wild animal to speak. She only stares at me—or at nothing—and keeps silent. If she understands anything I say to her, she gives no sign. I look into those blue eyes and am certain she does not want to be here with us. I have no idea where to begin.

CHAPTER TWO

*N*aduah watched the girl with yellow hair and eyes the color of the sky. The girl smiled as the meaningless sounds streamed from her mouth. It was a strange tongue that seemed familiar but beyond understanding, from some other time. The girl pointed her finger, saying "You, Sinty-ann." Then she pointed to herself and said, "Me, Loo-see."

Sinty-ann: the name called her by White Hair, the old man who came and took her from the soldiers' camp. That name, *Sinty-ann*, part of the speech White Hair made, were the only sounds she recognized. It was her name in the other time, before her life with the People, in the time when she was still a child. It sounded odd to her ears, not like the name the People had given her: *Naduah*. She pointed to herself, as the girl Loo-see had, and said, "Naduah."

7

Loo-see frowned. "Naduah?" She shook her head. Then she took the woman's hard, rough hand in her own soft one and placed the hand against the woman's chest. "Sinty-ann," she repeated. "Say, 'My—name—is—Sinty—ann.'"

Naduah said nothing. She would not speak their name for her again. The smile on Loo-see's face faded. Then the baby stirred awake in Naduah's lap and began to murmur. Loo-see pointed to the little girl, her face making a question. Naduah understood what she was asking: *What is her name?*

"Topsannah," she answered.

"Topsannah," Loo-see repeated, nodding. "Topsannah." She did the finger-pointing again. "Me, Loo-see. Her, Topsannah. You, Sinty-ann."

Then someone called in a voice like a crow's, and Loo-see hurried away. When she had gone, Naduah fumbled open the shirt they had given her—she wasn't used to buttons—and nursed the child.

For a few minutes she was alone and had time to think. She hadn't been by herself since they brought her to this place. When she was with the People, she was hardly ever alone, but here it was different. The white strangers came and looked at her. The women clasped their hands together under their chins and spoke to each other about her. Their light eyes darted back to stare at her again and again. Some would step forward, putting their faces close to hers and speaking loudly, as though that would make her understand.

She stopped trying to speak to them in her language, to tell them that somewhere, days and nights of hard riding from here, was her family: two sons, Quanah and Pecos, no longer children but young braves who rode their own fast ponies and were skilled with bow and arrow, already warriors like their father. And Peta Nocona, her husband, a chief. These white people refused to understand that she must go back to them.

The white men's attack had been completely unexpected. She and the other women had been in the camp near the river with their children. Most of the men of the tribe were away on a buffalo hunt. It was the end of the big hunting season when the great animals were in their thick winter fur. The tribe had not yet taken as much meat as they needed to last them through the long winter, and the men had decided to make one more hunt before the snow came. While they were away, the white men rode in with roaring guns.

Naduah had seen white men before. Sometimes traders came from the west, speaking still another strange tongue, the language of the People's Mexican slaves. (She knew a few words of the slaves' language.) It was different from what these new white men spoke. The traders brought blankets and iron kettles and coffee and other things the People wanted. They exchanged them for the strings of horses and herds of cattle the warriors had taken in raids, and for buffalo skins not needed for tipis and clothing. Naduah was used to those white men, and the People got on well with them.

White men sometimes came from the east, too, men like those who had attacked the camp. Twice these white men had come to the People, once when she was a young girl not yet married, and later, when her sons were small, barely out of their cradleboards. The white men had told the People that they wanted her to come back with them, offering to give mules and other valuable gifts if the People would let her go.

The first time, when she was still a young girl, she had

been too frightened to speak to the white men, or even to know what she should do. Speckled Eagle, the man she called Father, refused the gifts and sent the white men away.

The second time she was much older. When someone explained to her what the men wanted, Naduah, herself, refused to go with them. They had nothing to do with her, these men with their pale skins and strange way of talking. She had a husband and young sons. She would stay with the People, where she belonged. She knew the white men were angry, but they could do nothing and they, too, went away. She did not see any white men again until her sons were older and she had borne a daughter.

At the time of the last new moon, many white men on horseback rode into the camp, taking the People by surprise. They began shooting at the women and children, perhaps mistaking them for men in the noise and confusion and swirling dust, perhaps not. Naduah and the other women leapt on their ponies and tried to flee. Topsannah, hidden beneath Naduah's buffalo robe, clung to her.

The only young man in the camp that day was her husband's Mexican slave. Naduah saw him shot dead as he rushed to help her. She managed to elude two of her pursuers, but a third took aim and fired at her horse. She jumped from the pony as it fell, certain that they would shoot her as well.

Her robe dropped from her shoulders, and when the men realized that this was a woman with a child, they held their fire. She started to run, but the men were on horseback and quickly caught her. One of them seized her roughly by the shoulders. When he turned her around and saw that her eyes were light like his own, he called the others to come and look.

They put her and the child on one of their horses, and while the other white men took what they wanted from the camp and set fire to what was left, led them away—away from her husband and sons who would return from the hunt and find only desolation.

They traveled for four days and well into the nights. At first Naduah recognized the land over which they rode, land the People knew well, and she watched for a chance to escape. But there was never an opportunity. Guards were always posted around the horses, and she knew they would quickly recapture her if she tried to flee on foot.

On the fifth day they arrived at a soldiers' camp and took her to the wife of the chief of the soldiers. Naduah assumed that she would be beaten and made a slave; this is what the People would have done with a captive. But that did not happen.

With little cries and gestures the wife and another woman took away Naduah's buckskin dress and leggings and winter moccasins. They dragged a tub in front of a fire blazing in the wall of the cabin and emptied kettles of steaming water into the tub. Then they coaxed her to climb into the water. She did not understand this; it was not something the People did. But as she obeyed and sat in the tub, a memory of her own small white body immersed in warm water and the face of a smiling, pale-eyed woman hovering over her flitted through her mind. *Her mother? Had her mother in the time before the People done this?*

The white women poured more warm water over her head and rubbed something into her hair. The juice ran down over her face and stung her eyes. They took away the baby's rabbit skin and breechcloth and handed her to Naduah, showing with gestures that she was to wash the baby. And when they allowed her to climb out, the women dried them both with blankets and gave them clothes to put on. Not her own buckskin but a dress made of cloth.

The dress was too small. Naduah was a tall woman, broad-shouldered and wide-hipped, muscular from hard work. The women made her understand she would have to wear the bad-fitting dress anyway. Their leather foot-covers pinched her feet, but her moccasins were gone, along with her clothes. They would not let her have the buffalo robe. Instead they brought her a woolen blanket, like those the People sometimes got from the traders. It was not as heavy as the buffalo robe, and not as warm.

They did the same for the baby: her rabbit skin disappeared and a dress was put on her. The little girl whimpered in protest and clutched at her mother.

Then the women combed Naduah's light brown hair, fastening it back away from her face. She reached up to touch it. It felt odd without the bear grease she used to rub on it.

They offered her food, but it looked and smelled strange —tasted strange, too. She ate only because she needed strength to nurse Topsannah.

After she had been at the soldiers' camp for many days, kept in a small, bare room and brought food from time to time, White Hair came. He made them let her out of the small room and looked her over carefully. Then he spoke her old name, Sinty-ann. It startled her to hear that name. When he saw that she recognized the sounds, he became very agitated, and tears came to his eyes.

With him was a man who knew some of the People's language, and Naduah tried to tell this man that she must go back to her People, that she must find her sons and her husband. But they both shook their heads no. After that she said nothing more. It was useless.

White Hair put her and the child in a wagon drawn by two mules. They were accompanied by several men on horseback. One was the man who knew the words of her People and tried to make her speak to him. Another she recognized as one of those who had attacked the camp and captured her, a young man with hair growing on his lip beneath his nose. Men of the People did not have hair on their faces. They plucked it all out, even the short hairs that sprouted on the brow above the eyes. They would have laughed at this Hair Beneath His Nose. He rode a chestnut mare, a fine horse, but they also would have laughed at a man riding a mare.

She had no idea where they were taking her. Instead of heading north, the direction from which the soldiers had brought her, they rode toward the rising sun. All day they traveled, a slow, bumpy journey along a rough trail that took her farther from her People. If she could not go to them, she thought, perhaps the People would find her. She clung to that hope as long as she could. But as White Hair and the others continued their eastward journey, hope began to fade.

The People had nothing like this wagon. Everyone rode horses, even young children, and they moved their goods with pack horses and mules, each dragging two long tipi poles tied to the saddle, their tipi skins and other belongings slung between the poles. She would have preferred riding one of the mules that pulled this wagon to being jolted on the rough wooden seat.

At night they camped, unrolling their blankets beneath the wagon. One of the men was always posted as a guard. To keep them from being attacked or to keep her from running away? She did not know. She half dreamed, half remembered: *Long ago in the other time, a wagon much bigger than this one with a cover over it, crossing rivers and plains for many days, going to the new place, Mother and Father and others, two brothers, then a sister. What were their names? Me—Sinty-ann. And the brothers—John, was that one of them?*

After a few days, White Hair and the others brought her to a big log cabin. More strangers poured out to greet her. More noise, more talk in the strange tongue with its faintly familiar sounds: *Sinty-ann, Sinty-ann.* They led her inside, hovering close, smiling, staring, talking loudly.

Holding Topsannah tightly, she looked around, half-curious, half-frightened. The cabin had two large rooms joined by an open hallway with a steeply pitched roof that covered the broad gallery. The rooms were filled with strange objects, uncomfortable to sit on, she found, and worse to lie on. The first night they insisted that she sleep on a soft mattress of feathers laid on a web of ropes strung on a wooden frame, but she took the blankets from the bed and spread them on the wooden floor.

She missed her tipi of lodgepoles set in a circle and tied together at the top, covered with buffalo hides she had tanned and stitched herself. Thick buffalo robes on the inside kept cold drafts from coming in, and a small pit fire in the center warmed them better than this fire in a stone part of the wall.

She missed her sleeping skins piled on a bed of dried grass.

The white women gave her more strange things to eat and drink, and all of them talked to her, asking her questions she did not understand, waiting for her answer, but never listening to *her* questions: *Where are my sons? Where is my husband? When can I go to them?*

The girl called Loo-see lived in this cabin with White Hair and people Naduah thought must be her parents and brothers and sisters. When the others had finished with their questions, Loo-see gently led Naduah around the cabin, pointing to things and saying their names: table . . . stool . . . fire . . . lamp . . . kettle. Loo-see seemed kind, not loud-speaking like the others, but not even to please her would Naduah try to imitate the sounds Loo-see made.

Then Loo-see took her outside and showed her other, smaller buildings near the big cabin: a smokehouse with haunches of meat hanging inside, a corncrib half-filled with dried ears from the fall harvest, a springhouse where they got their water. In the distance at the edge of the fields was a small, crude cabin. "That's where Grandfather's Negroes live," Loo-see explained.

Naduah looked for the place where the horses were kept and easily found a long shed with a corral. As soon as she could, she would take two or three of the sleek, well-fed horses and go in search of the People.

She knew it was a long way. This place was not familiar, but she would ride toward the setting sun until she recognized where she was. She had no bow and arrow with which to shoot game along the way; she would have to take some of the white people's strange food, and, if necessary, kill one of the horses, as the men in her tribe did when they needed food as they traveled. She would watch carefully for her chance.

Loo-see, her mother, and her sister Mar-ta, a tall, thin girl with yellow hair and blue eyes like Loo-see's, prepared a large meal. They set food in bowls on the wooden table. Loo-see's family took their places around the table on benches and stools with three legs, a little girl and a little boy and an older boy with one arm missing seated on one side with the mother, Loo-see and Mar-ta on the other side with the father. White Hair sat at one end, and Naduah and Topsannah were placed at the other in what she understood was a seat of honor. Hands together, heads bowed, they were silent while White Hair spoke, his eyes closed. She heard their name for her, "Sinty-ann."

Then Loo-see's mother, a stern-faced woman with a thin, pinched mouth, took meat and other food from the bowls and put it on plates, which she set in front of each one. "Beef," she said, pointing to the meat.

Naduah had eaten beef, often stolen in raids on farmers like these. She preferred buffalo, but she reached out and picked up a piece of meat in her hand.

"Sinty-ann," said Loo-see's mother, "use your fork. Like this." She held up a metal tool with sharp points.

Naduah was not accustomed to tables and plates and such tools. The People used knives to cut chunks of meat that had been speared on a green stick to cook over a fire or boiled in a pot. They sat on the ground to eat and held the food in their hands or on stiff pieces of hide or bark. Awkwardly, Naduah tried to use the tool.

White Hair sliced the large, soft lump in front of him and

passed the pieces to Loo-see's sisters and brothers. "Bread," the little boy said, watching her with narrowed eyes.

This, too, was strange. She laid the slice on her plate and tried to eat it with the metal tool as they wanted her to eat the meat. The younger children laughed, covering their mouths with their hands. Then she saw that the bread was not eaten with the metal tool but held in the hand. It was soft, spread with some kind of fat—butter, they called it. Odd, but it tasted good. Yet as she chewed it, she remembered: *Mother—putting something in the oven, taking something out, puffed and brown. Did she call it bread?* This bread would be good to take with her, to eat on the journey. She knew there was more of it hidden in a cupboard.

The younger boy and girl ate without taking their eyes off her, ready to laugh, although the parents spoke to them sternly when they did. Topsannah laughed when the children laughed. She seemed to like them, and later, when they had finished eating and Loo-see was putting the dishes into water, they played with her. Not knowing what else to do, Naduah sat watching them. Then she heard them call her baby by a strange name: Tecks Ann.

"Tecks Ann?" Naduah repeated.

"We don't like that old Indian name," the little boy, James, said. "We gave her a new name. We call her Tecks Ann."

"Name—is—Topsannah," Naduah said carefully.

They all looked at Naduah in surprise, and Loo-see wiped her hands and clapped them in pleasure. "Listen, she's learning, she's remembering English!"

They praised her and then went on with their work. Topsannah crawled up on her lap and whispered, "Tecks Ann."

She decided she would not tell anyone else her own name: Naduah. She would teach it to Topsannah, but that was all. And when they called her Sinty-ann, she would respond, but she would not say that name herself.

Toward sunset some nights and days after she had been brought here, she saw the chestnut mare again, not in the corral with the other horses but tied up outside the cabin. Maybe this was her chance to escape. Maybe she could simply grab the child and flee on that horse, taking the risk of finding food along the way. If she found nothing, she was used to going without food; the People had had many hard times in past winters. Hunger was nothing new to her.

Hair Beneath His Nose had come to visit Mar-ta. "That's Jedediah," Loo-see told her. "He and Martha are engaged to be married."

Naduah did not understand all of Loo-see's words, but she understood the look that passed between the girl and the young man. That did not interest her. She and the man looked at each other warily. The horse that waited outside was the one he had been riding when he helped to capture her. That was the horse she would take, with pleasure.

That night when the cabin was dark and she was certain the others slept soundly, Naduah wrapped herself and her sleeping child in whatever blankets she could find. Moving silently, she gathered two loaves of bread and a knife from the cupboard and tied them in a bundle. Then she crept outside.

The handsome horse was still there. It had not been put in the corral with the other horses. She laid her hand on the animal's nose and spoke quietly to it, calming it. Then quickly, as she had done many times with her own horses, she untied it and sprang up on its bare back, hugging the baby to her chest. There was probably a saddle in the shed, but she didn't need to look for it. She was used to riding without one, to directing a horse with the pressure of her legs and leather reins she had braided herself. But this horse had not been as carefully trained as the People's ponies, and it did not know how to respond as well as it should. Still, it was a strong horse, and she thumped it with her heels to urge it across the hard-packed earth.

She glanced at the sky and saw that the horns of the new moon pointed up. That meant rain, or even snow. It meant her trail could be easily followed in the damp earth. She would have to press the horse to its limit to keep ahead of those she knew would pursue her.

She was accustomed to riding hard. After a raid on a white settlement or on an enemy tribe, the People drove their ponies furiously, putting as much distance as possible between themselves and their enemies. Only much later when they believed it was safe did they allow themselves and their horses to rest. She had been on many raids with her husband. She had ridden as hard as he had.

During the night she and Topsannah headed straight into the teeth of a harsh wind that swept across the plains. Clouds gathered, covering the moon, and it began to snow. Fine swirling, needle-sharp flakes stung her face. Naduah wished she had her buffalo robe to keep them warm and dry, but that foolish woman at the soldiers' camp had taken it from her and kept it. She wished it not for herself, but for the child, awake now and crying with cold.

CHAPTER THREE

From Lucy Parker's journal, February 9, 1861

I truly believed we were making great progress with Cynthia Ann, but now I see that I was wrong. Just as I began to hope that we will succeed in civilizing her, something dreadful happened.

Three nights ago Cynthia Ann stole Jed's horse and rode off with Topsannah while everyone was asleep! Of course they found her the next day. It had snowed during the night, so her trail was easy to follow. She had traveled quite a long distance, but the cold must have been too much for her, or maybe for Topsannah, and she had stopped to make a fire.

Papa and Jedediah and my brother Ben brought them back wet and shivering with cold. We were all quite shocked that she would do such a thing, although I was less surprised than the others because I can see her deep unhappiness. Now

Grandfather says someone must watch her night and day, and the "someone" turns out to be me during the daytime. I do not enjoy the idea of being a jailer, but I suppose it must be, at least until she comes to accept that she must stay here with us and gives up her idea of returning to the Indians. If she ever does!

This event spoiled Martha's visit from Jedediah. He is busy with the Rangers, protecting our settlements from the depredations of the Indians, and has little time to stop with us. He talks of resigning soon, as does his friend Capt. Sul Ross. This is no life, he says, once the excitement is over. Jedediah dreams of becoming a merchant, a business he feels would be profitable with all the new people moving into Texas from the east.

Martha has confided to me that they plan to marry in October, after her sixteenth birthday and after the cotton crop has been brought in. I am to say nothing to anyone until Jedediah has spoken to Papa. I am quite excited at the idea of a wedding in the family, although I cannot bear the thought that Martha will be leaving us.

Last evening Papa pressed Jed for details about the attack on the Comanche camp up at Pease River. He has told us little, except to say that he believes Cynthia Ann's husband was a war chief much respected by his tribe. Capt. Ross claims to have shot and killed this warrior, Peta Nocona, but Jed is not certain of that. He says he is sure there were fewer men in the camp than some Rangers claim, that perhaps most of them were off on a hunt and the chief may not have been there at all. I do hope for Cynthia Ann's sake that her husband is not dead, although the world is surely better off without him. As Papa says, "The only good Indian is a dead Indian."

My brother Ben hangs on Jedediah's every word, because he is determined to be an Indian fighter when he is old enough, even though crippled by the loss of an arm from a rattlesnake bite. Martha is more tenderhearted. "But I cannot believe your men would shoot helpless women and children," she cried, thinking, I am sure, of Cynthia Ann being fired upon and nearly killed by her own people, after all these years.

"There is nothing helpless about those women," Jedediah said, his voice turning hard. "They can ride and shoot as well as the men, and they're just as fiendish. There will be no peace on the frontier until we've gotten rid of every last one of those red devils." I could see Ben nodding vigorously in agreement.

These seemed like such harsh words, but Papa reminds us that our people have suffered greatly from atrocities committed by the Indians. Our own family was nearly destroyed: my great-grandfather Elder John Parker scalped and mutilated, my great-uncles the same, including Cynthia Ann's father. Grandfather was indeed fortunate to escape harm. Two of his sisters-in-law were captured and treated horribly. And look now at Cynthia Ann! Mama and Papa believe that her mind has been forever destroyed by the harsh experiences of her capture and the years of living among savages. But we do not say this to Grandfather, who insists that our kindness and good care eventually will heal her.

Mama and Martha have decided that it will be better if Cynthia Ann learns useful work and that perhaps she will remember some English if she is kept busy with us. And so this morning, as the day was unusually mild and sunny for this time of year, we washed our clothes. We filled the tubs outside with water, and then we showed her how to work the clothes and bedclothes in the soapy water with a wooden stick. She is a strong and able worker, but she seemed to have no understanding of what we were trying to accomplish.

"Surely she has done this in her home!" I whispered to Mama, who said grimly, "Surely *not*, Lucy! Those barbarians never wash themselves, never clean their clothes. And I'm told their camps are so filthy they have to move often because it gets to smelling so bad. Mrs. Evans sent word from Fort Cooper that the poor thing arrived there full of lice. She destroyed all of Cynthia Ann's clothes, except for the buffalo robe, which she tried to wash. She thinks it might be made clean again if left outside in the sunshine."

It makes me shudder to think of that! How could any white child forget every bit of her upbringing and turn into a filthy savage? That is one question I ask myself. I look at my own younger sister, Sarah, who is a happy little girl, as Cynthia Ann must have been, always glad to help us with our chores. It pains me to think that something so sickening could have happened to such a young and innocent person.

Does Cynthia Ann remember those happy times with her family? She gives no sign. I see her watching our Sarah run and play, and I wonder what thoughts are in her mind. If she does remember, I hope her memories are of those early, happy days and not of the cruel ones that followed her capture. We have heard stories that captives are treated brutally. Papa, Mama, and Grandfather will not tell me what sorts of horrors they are made to suffer, and I frankly cannot imagine what they might be.

Grandfather has brought us a length of good blue calico so that Cynthia Ann may begin to learn to sew and make clothes for herself, as nothing of ours fits her properly. Mama has no patience for this, and so I suppose it will fall upon me to instruct her. It is logical, for I am the one who spends the most time with her as her "guard." I wonder if she knows that is my duty.

Slowly we are teaching Cynthia Ann what it is to be a white woman and to do the kind of chores a white woman does. As we work together, I make it my business to say the words of each thing that we do, and she has begun to repeat them after me, but very reluctantly. Often her mind seems far away, as though she does not hear me. Other times she seems to remember words from long ago and the language comes back to her in fits and starts.

Many of the things that we take for granted she appears not to know. She has never baked bread, that much is plain, for yesterday we showed her how to knead the dough, and she seemed mystified by its rising. Has she never seen a butter churn? I guess not, although according to Grandfather the Comanches have stolen many of the farmers' cattle, herding them right out from under our neighbors' noses and driving them west across the border into New Mexico to sell to the *Comancheros*, the Spanish-speaking traders. But with all those cows, it seems the raiding Indians did not bother to milk them, let alone to turn the milk into butter.

The strangest thing happened after Cynthia Ann had churned the cream and worked the curds in a bowl with the paddle until she had a crock of butter ready to take to the springhouse. She asked for some, and we gave it to her, thinking she wanted it to spread on the bread just taken out of the oven. Instead, *she put the butter on her hair!*

This made an awful mess and quite upset Mama, who is convinced that Cynthia Ann is truly, hopelessly mad. "If she continues to behave like this," she complains to Grandfather, "I don't know what I will do."

"We must pray for her, Anna" is his reply. This is always his response to our problems. Grandfather is determined that Cynthia Ann will become a Christian again, as she was as a small child. Each night he gathers us together and reads aloud from the Bible, hoping, I suppose, that the words themselves will affect her. And keep her from buttering her hair.

CHAPTER FOUR

*L*oo-see draped the length of dark blue cloth around Naduah's body and held it while Loo-see's Ma-ma marked it with a white stick. Then they spread the cloth on the table and cut it with two knives connected in the middle. Naduah had seen this doubleknife among the goods the traders offered the People, but it hadn't interested her. Now she saw how the thing worked, opening and closing to cut. Loo-see began to sew the pieces of cloth together.

Loo-see showed her a tiny metal tool with a very fine cord looped through a hole in one end. "Needle," Loo-see said. "Thread." She began to push the needle in and out of the cloth, drawing the thread through. "This is called sewing."

Naduah watched for a while and then took the cloth and needle from Loo-see. This she understood. She continued sewing the seam Loo-see had started, struggling to make her stitches as small and neat as Loo-see's. The little needle seemed clumsy in her big fingers.

Naduah had always made her family's clothes from the skins of deer and antelope that she had prepared herself. Sewing cloth took less effort, she found, than stitching skins. When she and the other women made their buckskin dresses with the long, rippling fringes that moved so gracefully when they walked, first each hole had to be punched in the leather with an awl, a bit of bone sharpened to a point. Then a length of sinew, taken from along the backbone of a buffalo, was poked and pulled through the holes with the fingers. It was slow, tedious work for the women, who made their tipis as well as all the clothing for their families.

Now, leaning close to a flickering lamp in the dim cabin and working the tiny needle in and out, like a fish swimming through water, Naduah remembered things she had almost forgotten.

She remembered the time when she was young, like Sarah, and new to the People. She was a slave then, sent to live with Calls Louder, wife of Speckled Eagle. The old woman shouted at her fiercely and made her cry when she did something wrong. She had to gather sticks and fetch water and do hard work, much harder than she had ever done before. Sometimes Calls Louder hit her, but more often she simply yelled at her. Then one day Calls Louder handed her a piece of buckskin and an awl and a bit of sinew and showed her what to do.

She was clumsy at first, even clumsier than she was now with this tiny needle and tiny stitches. Calls Louder was not patient, as Loo-see was. The Comanche woman slapped her and made her do it over and over until finally Naduah learned to sew well enough to please the old woman. The other girls her age—Sarah's age—were learning, too, but not as fast as she was, because they were children of the People, not slaves, and their lives were different, better than hers. She had not always been one of the People, she remembered now, although she had nearly forgotten the time when she was not.

Naduah sewed steadily on the blue calico, searching for other things to remember. First there was that life before the People, and then she was with the People and was a slave. But how did she get there, among the People? She did not know. Her life had been one way, and then it was another. Her memory would creep up close to what had happened to change her life and who she was, but it always slipped away before she could grasp it.

It was easier to remember her life after she had been with the People for a while, when she was no longer a slave but a member of Speckled Eagle's family. Speckled Eagle was a respected hunter and warrior, and she had come to think of him as her father. There were other children in the family, mostly older, a few younger. Father had two wives, Calls Louder and Walking At Night. Calls Louder was old and mean, but Walking At Night, the second, younger wife, was not so mean. Yet when it came right down to it, Calls Louder took better care of her, taught her more of what it meant to be a woman of the People. They had given her her name, Naduah: *She Who Carries Herself With Dignity And Grace.*

There was much to learn, and Naduah learned it well. Maybe it was after she was able to understand their tongue and to speak it that she was no longer a slave but one of them.

She could make clothing, of course, and she had gained a reputation in the tribe for making the best tipi covers. Some of the women even came to her to ask for help when it was time to prepare the buffalo hides for their tipis.

She knew how to pick lodgepoles that were long and straight, and how to stitch together the hides to fit over the poles, more than the number of fingers on both hands. She was quick at setting up the tipi with the low entrance facing the rising sun and the smokehole above it, and just as quick at striking the tipi when the time came to move.

She was good on a horse, too, almost as good as the men, and she could use a bow and arrow accurately. Although some women were stronger, she could outrun them all. She was taller, her legs longer. She was skillful with a knife, good at cutting the buffalo meat into strips for drying. Her family always had plenty of food, with enough left over to give to those who had less, and plenty of well-made, good-looking clothes. But she was not good at painting the designs on her warrior-husband's buffalo robes. For that she went to one of Walking At Night's sisters to ask that it be done.

Now Naduah watched Topsannah go off to play with Sarah, holding on to Sarah's hand, although it made the mother uneasy when the child was out of her sight. The little girl answered when they called her Tecks Ann, and she seemed to be using some of their language. Now Ma-ma got angry when Naduah spoke to the child in her own tongue.

"Don't talk Indian," the woman said sternly. "We speak English here."

More and more of what these white people said was beginning to make sense to Naduah. Some of it was Loo-see's careful, tireless teaching; some of it was her own memory awakening. But she would not let them know how much she understood, and she would not speak the language except to repeat the words Loo-see taught her for the work she was given to do, or for things she needed: butter . . . quilt . . . bread . . . and this word for the doubleknife, scissors.

One white man's word she had known all along and did not have to be taught was *horse*, a word used often by the traders. The horse was the center of the People's life. The horse meant wealth, power, freedom. Sometimes they called it the god-dog, because—as Speckled Eagle explained to her—it did the work that dogs used to do, hauling heavy loads when the camp was moved. But it could find its own food in a way that a dog could not.

These people—White Hair and the others who insisted they were her family—were afraid she would try to run away again, and they made sure she was never alone for very long. One day while she was sewing, a visitor had stopped at the farm, a white man. She paid no attention until they brought him in and allowed her to meet this man they called Coho.

"He was a captive," White Hair explained. "Like you. Talk to him. Ask him about your family."

She didn't like the look of this man, didn't trust him, even though he spoke to her in the language of the People. He seemed to know nothing about her husband or children.

"Will you help me?" she whispered, thinking it was foolish not to take the chance. "Steal a horse for me and guide me back. My husband will repay you, I promise you."

This Coho shook his head. "Can't do that," he said.

"Please," she begged, trying to keep her voice calm so that

White Hair and the others would think she was asking simple questions. "My heart cries all the time for my sons."

The man turned away from her and spoke to White Hair in the white man's language. "She says she wants to go back. I'd keep my eye on her, if I was you."

And they did. It seemed that Loo-see was always with her now, and Naduah had to think of ways to get Loo-see to visit the corral. The horses white men rode were much larger than the mustang ponies the People preferred for their speed and endurance. But it was just such horses as these that the People seized in their raids; stolen horses were a mark of prestige, a sign of a man's cleverness.

Naduah's husband, Peta Nocona, had distinguished himself in the tribe as a raider, as well as a hunter and a warrior. Where was he now? And her son Quanah, who like his father never seemed to know fear, what had become of him? Or of Pecos, not very strong but still brave? Did they yearn for her as she did for them? She bent over her sewing so that Loo-see and the others would not see her face. These white people seemed to have no understanding of her loss, of the pain she suffered being away from her family—her real family.

Lying nearby on the table was the doubleknife, the scissors, that Loo-see and Ma-ma had been using to cut cloth. Naduah glanced around, and when she was sure no one was looking, she slipped the scissors into her pocket. Then she stood up.

"Privy," she said.

They smiled and nodded approvingly when she used one of their words. Throwing a blanket around her shoulders, she walked quickly toward the little wooden shack a short distance from the cabin. How strange these white people were, making a special place for these things, instead of simply using the bushes, as the People did. She knew that Ma-ma had opened the cabin door a little way and was watching her to make sure she was going where she said she was.

Once inside the privy with the door latched, Naduah pulled out the pins that Ma-ma had stuck in her hair, and her light locks fell loosely to her shoulders. Weeping, she seized a lock, drew out the scissors, and hacked at it. She dropped fistfuls of her hair through the hole in the wooden seat until most of it was chopped off.

Still weeping, she unbuttoned her shirtwaist and chemise, exposing her breasts, and dragged the point of the scissors across her skin, making long, deep cuts in her flesh until it bled. The pain she felt was nothing compared to her grief.

Cutting the hair, cutting the flesh—this was what the women of the People did when they were in mourning. The white people didn't understand that she was in mourning, and she didn't expect them to understand this, either. She could not hide the hair from them, but they would never know about her breasts.

Feeling calmer, she wiped the blades of the doubleknife and put it in her pocket. She walked back to the cabin, the blanket pulled up over her head, her face a stony mask.

At first no one noticed. Naduah quietly laid the scissors on the table again and resumed her sewing. Then White Hair and Loo-see's father and brother, Ben, came in from the fields, Ben's empty shirt sleeve pinned up. She felt White Hair's eyes resting on her, heard him suck in his breath. "What in God's name has she done to herself?" he whispered.

Everyone turned and stared at her, and then they all began

to speak at once. Naduah held her sewing in her lap and waited for whatever was going to happen.

"She's cut her hair!" Loo-see cried. "Oh, Sinty-ann, your beautiful hair!"

"See there!" Ma-ma said. "I *told* you!"

"Quiet, all of you!" White Hair thundered. But when he spoke again, it was in a gentle voice. "Sinty-ann?" he said, and she glanced up at the sound of the name. "How are you?" he asked, speaking slowly. "Are you well?"

She understood him, the sense of what he was saying, but she refused to let herself show that she understood. She lowered her eyes again to the cloth in her hands.

"She was doing much better," she heard Loo-see say tearfully. "She's learning new words every day. I cannot imagine what possessed her—"

"Does she speak?"

"That takes time. And she works hard," Loo-see added quickly. "She's learning to sew, quite nicely, too, and we've taught her to make bread."

The old man was silent. "I wonder what she's thinking," he said. "All those years with those savages. You have to ask yourself what made her stay with them, to live a life like that."

"Well, *I* know the answer to that," Ben said, his mouth a hard, straight line. "All you have to do is look at her. She's turned savage, too, just like them!"

CHAPTER FIVE

From Lucy Parker's journal, February 18, 1861

When will it stop getting worse? Yesterday while we sewed, Cynthia Ann took Mama's scissors and slipped out to the privy, where she chopped off most of her hair. I cannot imagine why she would do such a thing, and there is no way to get her to explain. Grandfather wants to bring Mr. Mason again to speak to her in Comanche, but I believe that is useless, that there are things she will not tell us in any language. The one thing needing no explanation is her unhappiness.

I suspect that she understands far more than she lets on, but so far she speaks only those words I teach her about our life here. I know nothing about her life *there*, before she came to us, although I dream that someday she will find her own words to tell me.

Everything seems so strange to her—our furniture, for example. When I see that even a plain wooden stool is unfamiliar, I cannot help but wonder what other things so common in our lives are unheard-of in hers.

Our food is also strange and unappetizing to her. She eats because she is still nursing Topsannah, although that will likely soon end. She eats the beef we serve on special occasions, but clearly does not like pork, our most plentiful meat, or chicken, whether stewed or roasted, and wants nothing to do with the eggs fresh from our henhouse. She will eat dried corn prepared in various ways—hominy, hoecake, cornmeal mush—although Grandfather says that her people do not plant corn, in fact, do no farming at all. She is fond of sweet things, her favorite being Mama's berry preserves on a thick slice of bread.

Topsannah, on the other hand, is adjusting beautifully. She eats anything and everything, or at least agrees to a taste, and she seems to understand much of what we say to her. (I still call her Topsannah, for her mother's sake, although she answers to Tecks Ann.) We believe her to be about a year and a half old, and she is bright and cheerful. Just the opposite of her mother! It makes me curious about her father.

I asked Grandfather what he knows about Cynthia Ann's husband, and he said, "If that's what you want to call him! They don't marry, at least not like us. And he probably has several fat, dirty squaws. Some of those lazy bucks manage that, and it gives them more work than they can get out of one woman. Our poor Cynthia Ann was no doubt just one of them, with the most work to do."

Grandfather makes the man sound so repulsive. But if he was as bad as all that, how could she have stayed with him? Why did she not run away or agree to come back when the traders asked her to?

I cannot ask Mama that, because she says these are delicate matters and immediately changes the subject. When Jedediah was here on his last visit, I overheard him and Martha talking about Cynthia Ann and her husband, and I eavesdropped shamelessly:

"It is known that the Comanches are no better than animals and have no such thing as morals," Jed was saying.

"But she wants to go back to him! Why else does she try to run away? I believe she truly loves him."

"Love is what white people do, Martha," Jed told her. "Indians don't know about love. Get that romantic notion out of your head right now. All those savages know about is killing and stealing and taking captives, that's all they ever *will* know about, and the sooner we get rid of them all, every last one, the better it will be for every Texan trying to live in peace."

I strained to hear my sister's reply but could not make out her words.

"To tell you the truth, Martha," Jed went on, "I think your cousin Cynthia Ann is probably too far gone to be helped. She isn't white anymore. Except for those blue eyes, she doesn't look white, now does she? She's gone Indian, and that makes her no better than any of them. If I was your grandfather, I'd not only let her go, I'd take her back personally and consider myself well rid of her."

It was much more than I cared to hear, and I crept away from my listening place and hurried to help Mama with supper. Some of what Jedediah said may be true, about them being savages, but this much I know: whether she is Indian or white or some of both, our cousin's heart is surely broken.

CHAPTER SIX

*N*aduah sat on the long gallery that stretched across the front of Isaac Parker's double cabin, her sewing in her lap, watching Topsannah. The little girl squatted on short, sturdy legs, playing with a rag doll with yellow yarn hair tied in braids. Bright blue eyes and a smiling red mouth were stitched on the white muslin face. Loo-see had made the doll as a surprise for Topsannah, sewing it a little dress from scraps of the blue calico left from Naduah's dress and adding a white apron and a bonnet tied with ribbons. Topsannah jabbered to her doll, pretending to feed it as she had seen Sarah do with hers, but quickly she tired of that and brought the doll to her mother. Then she toddled off unsteadily to play with Sarah and James.

Naduah gazed at the doll. Somewhere back in the camp by the river, she remembered, there used to be a soft buckskin doll tied up in a miniature cradleboard. Calls Louder had made that doll for Topsannah. The doll had probably been destroyed when the soldiers burned the camp to ashes.

From the porch she could see the fields where, now that the weather was warming, White Hair and Pa-pa and Ben and their black-skinned slaves worked from sunrise to sunset. These men seemed strange to her, the way they spent their time, digging and planting, day after long day in the same place. Did they not get restless? Especially Ben, with the missing arm, who in some ways reminded her of her own sons but was so different. Would he and the other white men not have preferred to live by hunting, as the People did? Why did they choose to tie themselves down with these clumsy, uncomfortable log cabins when they could be free to go where the buffalo were plentiful, to live in tipis that could be taken wherever they wanted?

These women were lazy, Naduah thought. They would not have pleased warrior husbands. The work the white women did was not hard. But though their lives were much easier, they were like prisoners! She knew that her own life here was less arduous, but she, too, was a prisoner, and they seemed to have no understanding of that. They believed they were being good to her!

She missed her own work, her real work. When she thought of it, the endless chores no longer seemed burdensome. There was so little for her to do here that she had plenty of time to think, too much time to remember what her life had been like not so long ago. It made her sad.

Last night she saw that it was the time of the full moon. That was the time the war chiefs chose for their raids. Peta

Nocona would call the other men together and tell them his thoughts. If they agreed, the preparations began. Often, she remembered, the shields of the men were hung on racks outside the entrance to their tipi to soak up the power of the sun.

The night before the men left to make war, they would hold a war dance with singing and storytelling when the dancers rested. Everything was ready: a little food for emergencies, bows and arrows—not the kind of arrows used for hunting, which could be used over and over again, but a special kind that was left in the dead enemy—lances, tomahawks. Sometimes Naduah went along; sometimes, if the enemy target was far away, the other women went, too, to set up a temporary camp.

The scouts would already have gone ahead. The next morning the warriors would leave, riding steadily, quietly, stopping once at midday to rest and take care of their horses. At night they camped around a small fire, passing the sacred pipe. The chief traveled with his warbonnet safe in a buckskin case, ready to put on when the battle began.

When they approached a settlement—like this one, Naduah thought—a small group would dash in furiously in broad daylight, whooping and screaming, taking their victims by surprise. They seized what they wanted—usually horses—killed the men, and scalped them, snatched any children they could find, and raced away.

They would ride into the village in their war paint. That night they would celebrate with a victory dance, with a huge bonfire, the men and women dressed in their finest clothes. The warriors waved the scalps they had taken, the skin stitched to a hoop of willow twig. When it was a successful raid with lots of plunder, the dancing sometimes lasted for days.

When the raid was unsuccessful, it was a different matter. Warriors lost their lives and there was no loot to show for the effort. Naduah remembered the wailing and frenzied mourning of the women that sometimes went on for a long time.

Was there anyone mourning for her, Naduah wondered.

The moon had been nearly full when the white men captured her in the camp by the river. More full moons had come and gone. That was many days, although she did not know how to count them. She knew that as more days passed, as more moons waxed and waned, it would be harder for her to find her way back to the People again.

She felt these white people tried to do their best for her. It would have been easier to hate them if they had been cruel. She thought of Loo-see's eager, kind face as she tried to teach her useful things.

Naduah watched Loo-see walking across the yard from the corral with her grandfather, White Hair, who carried a bulky bundle under one arm. Naduah gazed past them into the distance, hoping, as always, to see horsemen, her People, riding toward them.

But then White Hair was climbing up on the gallery, smiling at her. "I have something for you, Sinty-ann," he said and laid the bundle at her feet.

She stared at it for a moment before she recognized it and seized it with a cry. Her buffalo robe! Sarah and Topsannah and James stopped playing and ran to look, and Ma-ma stepped out of the cabin, arms folded tightly across her chest.

"Oh, Mr. Parker!" Ma-ma cried, her voice like a crow. "Whatever did you bring that dirty thing here for!"

"It's all right, Anna," he said gruffly. "It's been scrubbed half to death by those women down at Fort Cooper. They wouldn't have sent it up here if it wasn't clean enough for you."

Carefully Naduah unfolded the heavy robe. It was all she had left of her life with the People. Ma-ma, mistrustful, kept her distance, but Loo-see was curious, like the children, wanting to see. The thick winter hair, almost as long as her arm from wrist to elbow, was worn on the inside of the hide. Proudly Naduah turned it over to show them the designs that had been painted on the back, proving that she was the wife of a great warrior and chief.

But the designs were gone. They had not completely disappeared but were so faded they were barely visible. This could not be! She had overseen the painting herself, watched as Walking At Night's sister had first painted the narrow line of vermilion down the middle to conceal the stitching where the two parts of the hide were joined. Then, following Naduah's wishes, she had pressed the colored powders into the skin with a piece of bone. To preserve the designs, Naduah herself had applied several thin coats of gluey sizing made from flesh scraped from the hide and boiled. Now all the scrubbing done by those women at the soldiers' camp had destroyed the designs that symbolized her husband's war honors, that counted the many coups he had struck in battle to show what a mighty chief he was. All gone!

It was too much. She could not hide her tears. Her only

comfort was that she had her robe again. It would keep her warm when she escaped.

"Buffalo," said Loo-see.

"Buffa," Topsannah repeated clearly. "Buffa, buffa!"

Naduah looked at her child, now learning the white people's language instead of her own, and her mind slipped away, far from this gloomy cabin, back to the harsh freedom of the Plains.

When she was young, endless herds of the humped, woolly beasts had covered the plains for as far as you could see. But after the white men began to hunt them for their skins, leaving the carcasses to rot, there were not as many as there had once been. The lives of the People depended on the buffalo; they hunted him in order to live. Sometimes there were not enough, and everyone was hungry.

She thought of the hunts.

The People watched the horned toads to see which way they hopped, they scanned the skies for ravens that circled above a herd waiting to gobble up the insects that thrived in the animals' hairy coats. Scouts followed these signs, and when they brought back word that a herd had been sighted, preparations began in the camp—bows were strung, arrows were tipped and feathered, racks were built for drying the meat.

When everything was ready, they held a dance. Drummers drummed, singers sang, men and women formed long lines facing each other and danced. They drummed and sang and danced half the night and then slept for a few hours until it was time for the hunters to leave.

The men rode out of the camp before dawn, wearing only

their breechcloths, following the directions of the scouts. Often it was Peta Nocona who led the hunt. Naduah sometimes went, too, riding her pony, bow and arrow ready to pick off a stray buffalo cow. Such excitement!

Moving against the wind—the buffalo had a keen sense of smell—and taking care to stay out of sight and hearing, the hunters surrounded the herd, forming a noose. When the signal was given, they rode in, tightening the noose. Threatened, sensing danger, the bulls began to circle, around and around, tighter and tighter, faster and faster, pushing the cows and calves toward the center.

When the right moment came, each hunter chose an animal and rode up close, aiming at the vulnerable spot between ribs and hip, so the arrow would reach the vital organs. Arrows flew fast and with tremendous force, and the enormous animals dropped to the ground while the horses swiftly sidestepped to avoid the horns of those that still ran.

Naduah and the other women rushed to be the first to touch a freshly killed buffalo and to find the ones that belonged to their men; each always knew her husband's arrows. Peta Nocona plunged his knife into his buffalo and pulled out the warm liver, spread it with the juice from the gallbladder, and shared it with his family. When that feast was over, the men skinned and butchered the animals, wrapping huge chunks of meat in hides to carry back to camp. Nearly every part of the animal was used. Only the heart was left behind in the cage of clean-picked ribs, to ensure that there would be more buffalo.

Then the women's work began: They sliced the meat into long, thin strips to dry on racks in the sun to make jerky. Then they pounded this jerky and mixed it with dried fruits and nuts and fat and sealed the pemmican in rawhide bags. They spent many more hours scraping the buffalo hides, working the skins until they were soft and supple, ready to use.

There were two seasons for hunting—when the warm weather came, the buffalo shed their long hair and the hides were at their best for making tipi covers and summer blankets, then again when the weather turned cold and the hair had grown long and thick. Every hunt meant hours and hours of exhausting labor for everyone until the work was done. Then the men would go out once more and hunt again, and there would be more meat, more hides, more work to make everything the People needed.

Topsannah's shriek pulled her back to the present. Naduah realized with a start that James had taken the robe and draped it fur-side out around his knobby little body. He was crawling around on the hard-packed earth after Topsannah, his fingers curled into horns. Topsannah danced merrily around him, her dark eyes shining. "Buffa! Buffa!" she cried.

"No!" Naduah leaped to her feet, snatching away the robe, and sent the boy sprawling. He made an ugly sound, and Topsannah burst into disappointed tears.

Naduah instantly regretted her action. The boy made her think of Pecos, her younger son, not as strong as Quanah but playful and quick. She reached out to comfort him, but he jerked away from her.

"You ain't white," he said angrily. "They might say so, but you ain't. You ain't nothing but a dirty old Indian." And he stomped off.

CHAPTER SEVEN

From Lucy Parker's journal, March 12, 1861

*M*uch excitement! Mama has told us a wonderful secret: she is expecting a baby late in the summer. And that is not all—Martha has announced that Papa has given his approval and she and Jedediah will be married in October.

For a wedding present, Grandfather has given them a piece of his land on which to build a log cabin and begin to farm. Grandfather believes there will be a war now that Texas has joined the South in seceding from the Union, a poor time in his judgment to begin a business in Fort Worth, as Jed had wanted. And so for the time being they have set aside their plans to move away. I am so happy that Martha will not be leaving us completely. And now there will be preparations for a wedding as well as a new baby. I have decided to make a quilt for Martha, although Mama says it is a bigger job than I realize.

I like my future brother-in-law well enough, although his attitude toward our poor Cynthia Ann, which he makes no effort to conceal, pains me. And Benjamin swallows whole everything Jed says! I have heard Jed say repeatedly that she has "gone Indian," which is no good at all. In his service with the Rangers he has been exposed to the savagery of the redskins, and he sees them as the very incarnation of evil. He believes that, given half a chance, Cynthia Ann would do us all great harm. I do not agree in the least, but it is useless to argue because Jed dismisses me as a child of twelve who knows nothing. I know more about our cousin than he ever will!

Grandfather turns a deaf ear to Jedediah's tirades. No matter what anyone says, Grandfather is endlessly patient with Cynthia Ann and urges us all to pray mightily and to hope for the best for her. He believes that she has been severely damaged by her years of captivity and that only by our loving kindness can she be restored to health of mind and spirit.

I must say, though, her body appears to be healthy enough! This morning I saw her pick up my father's ax and split a pile of logs for firewood. When Papa returned from planting corn, his logs were neatly split and stacked, and she was back in her place on the gallery, serenely sewing. Mama, who is the same age as Cynthia Ann and has worked hard all her life, is not nearly that strong.

Cynthia Ann seems determined to cling to as many of her old ways as we will allow. The buffalo robe, which Mrs. Evans scrubbed clean for her, is spoiled in Cynthia Ann's eyes. When she saw it, she burst into the most pitiable weeping and for a time was quite inconsolable. She sleeps on it now, and when she sews or does other work, she prefers to sit on it. How odd she looks squatting on that robe on our gallery! We have given up trying to persuade her otherwise, and it does seem harmless enough.

Somehow Cynthia Ann has become even more of a mystery to me than when she arrived here nearly two months ago. Why has she not become more like us? It's not that she doesn't know any better.

CHAPTER EIGHT

Naduah kneaded the mixture of flour, water, and starter (a bit of dough left from the last batch of bread they had made). Rhythmically folding and turning the warm lump of dough that stretched and shrank in her hands, she half listened to Loo-see's chatter. Something about Mar-ta. Something about Jed. It seemed that Loo-see's sister would become the wife of Hair Beneath His Nose, but not until many days would pass.

She remembered when she was a young girl, older than Loo-see but not as old as Mar-ta, and had been with the People for many seasons. She knew that her father, Speckled Eagle, thought it was time for her to have a husband. But he had been in no hurry to find one for her; he intended to be shrewd about it.

He had told her that she would fetch a fine bride-gift

because she was tall and well-made and strong, and it was known in the camp that she was a good worker. Speckled Eagle believed that several men were interested in having her for a wife. She had no choice in the matter, of course; it was up to her father and the man who wanted her most to reach an agreement.

She knew about this, because she had watched her older sister, Crooked Leg, daughter of Walking At Night, and had observed how she and other young women in the camp had gotten husbands. Naduah hoped that hers would not be an old man. Crooked Leg wound up with an old man even though she didn't want him. She became the youngest of his four wives, and the other wives made her life miserable, giving her all the hardest work to do.

Crooked Leg was angry when her father married her to the old man. She cried that she didn't want to go with him, but the old fellow had brought around several fine horses and left them outside Speckled Eagle's tipi, as was the custom. When her father saw them he immediately took them and put them in with his own herd. That settled it. The old man came by later and took Crooked Leg to his own tipi.

Of course the sisters still saw each other, but now Crooked Leg had a lot of work to do, more than when she was at home with her parents. Her husband's older wives made her do all the water carrying and wood gathering, and there was no time anymore to sit and talk. Being a wife was not like being a daughter, Crooked Leg told her unhappily.

Then one day Crooked Leg ran off with one of the handsome young braves, and when the couple came back after many days had passed, there was a lot of trouble. The young brave was whipped and forced to give the old man horses and other presents, and Crooked Leg's old husband had cut off the tip of her nose to teach her a lesson. Now no one else would want her, and she would have to stay with him.

Naduah made up her mind that she would not be stupid enough to do something that would result in losing part of her nose.

Then it was her time to marry. Crooked Leg, a gossip, had run all the way from the old man's lodge to tell Naduah what she had heard: Peta Nocona wanted Naduah for a wife.

Peta Nocona was old enough to have proved himself a capable hunter and raider. Already a chief because of his many successful raids, he had a reputation for stealing even the most carefully guarded horses from white men, slipping in and cutting loose the horses he wanted while their owners snored. As a warrior he had counted many coups in battle and had taken an impressive number of scalps. And so he had a good reputation and owned many horses, unlike the younger men who had not yet proved themselves nor accumulated enough wealth to secure a desirable wife. Peta Nocona would be able to provide plenty of meat and skins for his family, and he would be brave in battle. This would reflect well on her.

Yet he was far from old, and was fine looking, too: taller than Naduah, which was unusual because she was taller than all of the women of the People and most of the men as well. His long hair was thick and black, his lips were thin and straight, and his narrow nose arched like an eagle's beak.

Naduah could tell that Crooked Leg was envious. Not only was Peta Nocona the right age as well as being strong, respected, and also wealthy, but Naduah would be his first wife.

She would have the power and prestige no matter how many younger wives he took. She would be the one to carry his shield when they moved the camp.

Crooked Leg complained that if Speckled Eagle had not been in such a hurry to marry her off to the old man, Peta Nocona might have wanted to marry her, too, if not as his first wife then in a year or two as his second. Everybody knew it was better to take sisters as wives. They would get along better and not fight among themselves.

Naduah let her talk, not bothering to point out that Crooked Leg was the older sister, Naduah the younger. Peta Nocona would not have married the older sister after he had married the younger one.

The string of horses Peta Nocona led to Speckled Eagle's lodge were all excellent animals, but one of them was pure white, the rarest and finest of all. Of course her father knew all along that Peta Nocona had such a horse, and Peta Nocona must have known that Speckled Eagle admired it—there was not a man in the camp who did not want that horse.

There had not been much discussion about the arrangement. Calls Louder, Naduah's mother, was satisfied and did not put up her usual argument.

Speckled Eagle asked Naduah: Have you anything against this, daughter? She knew that if she did, she would be listened to. Perhaps not granted her wish, but heard, because she was now a favored daughter.

She said she did not.

Her father told her to take the gift horses to his herd— all but the white horse. That one would stay outside his lodge, Speckled Eagle added with a satisfied smile.

Before she left the tipi, she dressed in her best buckskin skirt with fine leather fringes swinging from the uneven hem and the seams, a buckskin blouse stitched with bands of red and black beads, and her finest moccasins. She streaked the part in her light brown hair with vermilion, and she painted her ears red on the inside, daubed her cheeks with orange circles, and took special care with the red and yellow stripes on her eyelids. Last, she put on her favorite necklace of bear claws, taken from bears Speckled Eagle had killed. Then she was ready, knowing that she looked good, as a woman of the People should.

When she came back from taking Peta Nocona's horses to her father's herd, the young chief was waiting for her. He was dressed up, too, in a long blue breechcloth with buckskin leggings and a shirt decorated with silver buttons and glass beads. She took a good look at his clothes. Until now his mother had made them for him and kept them in good condition, but after today it would be Naduah's job, and she knew she would do it well.

His long hair was parted in the middle and tied into two bunches, and he had painted a streak of yellow through his part. The scalp lock, combed from the crown of his head, was tied with eagle feathers. One side of his face was painted blue; the other side was decorated with yellow and white stripes. She was well pleased with him.

They nodded to each other, smiling, and she felt sure that he was pleased with her, too. She followed him to his tipi. Now she was his wife. She would carry his shield when the camp was moved and make certain it was in its place outside the entrance to their tipi. She was proud of the scalps on

Peta Nocona's shield, a sign that he was a great warrior.

But, like Crooked Leg, she had not realized how much work it was to be a wife, even though she had seen the women in her own family who seemed never to stop from the moment they awakened in the morning until they fell asleep at night. And there were two wives to please her father! Two of them—plus their own daughters—to prepare all the food and make all the clothes starting with the animal's skin, two of them to make the tipi covers and prepare for moving the camp and setting everything up in a new place, two of them to wait on him and tend to his wishes!

Each of Speckled Eagle's wives had her own tipi where she and her children slept. At night she tied a long leather thong to her wrist. The thong ran from her bed to her husband's, so that he could summon her whenever he wished during the night by yanking on it.

But Naduah was Peta Nocona's only wife, sharing his tipi with him and their children until their sons were old enough to move to their own separate tipis. There were times when she would have given a great deal for another wife to help her with her work, never imagining that someday her work would be taken away from her. Or that one day she would be making loaves of bread for this white family.

The first time Naduah saw the white women making bread, she had been astonished. It still seemed strange to watch the ball of dough swell up; when she punched it down, it would always rise again. What was this living thing that grew in the bowl? There was something in the dough that she did not understand, although they tried to explain it to her. It must be a spirit of some kind, she decided, like the spirits that dwelled in wild animals and in trees and rivers and hills. The People would be interested in this. She would take some to them, when she went back.

Making bread was the one thing she really liked to do. She enjoyed the taste of it, too. But it was the smell of it baking that summoned the memories of when she was very young, like Sarah, before she came to the People. Her mother had taught her to make this bread. In fact, had she not been making bread on that morning when—? *When what?* Her mind always went blank. She could not remember what it was that happened that morning—only the bread and its familiar, delicious smell.

As Loo-see stitched on her quilt and talked about her sister's wedding, Naduah patted the dough into loaves. She kept an eye on Topsannah, dressed in strange white people's clothes, playing white people's games with white children. How could her daughter learn the things she needed to know in order to be a wife of the People when both of them were prisoners here, so far from home?

The idea of escaping was never far from Naduah's mind. Her first attempt had been foolish; she had not planned carefully enough, and, of course, they had caught up with her and brought her back. After that there was always someone watching her—usually Loo-see during the day and the others taking turns at night—to make sure she did not try again. But time had passed, and they were no longer so careful. The days and nights were mild now, and she had the buffalo robe for protection if she needed it.

She knew well enough how dangerous such a journey would be. The main problem was food. Another was water. She would take what she could, but if the search for the People was long, there would be nothing more to eat when that food was gone. The cold weather was past, but this was still long before the plum bushes and grapevines and persimmon trees would bear fruit or the roots and bulbs and plants of the prairie would begin to grow. The People called this "The Season When Babies Cry for Food," because it was the time when their supply of buffalo jerky and pemmican was nearly exhausted, and all of them were hungry.

Even if she were well supplied, which way should she go? Some of the People could read the stars. Although she sometimes stared at the night skies above the cabin, they told her nothing. She would, she decided, ride in the direction of the setting sun where she would eventually find her way back to the People. Or they would find her.

And if she died out there on the vast, empty plains, it was better than dying here.

CHAPTER NINE

From Lucy Parker's journal, March 21, 1861

No sooner do I begin to feel more confident about Cynthia Ann, that she is truly finding contentment here among her family, than something terrible happens.

She ran away again. It was much the same as the last time—only this time she took Grandfather's gelding from the shed and two other horses, not ours. She took her buffalo robe, of course, and she supplied herself with several loaves of bread—she has learned to make it, and very good it is, too—and some jars of Mama's preserves. And, oddly enough, she also took our can of starter, as though she planned to bake more bread on her journey. Where she thought she would find flour, I cannot say.

This time the weather was favorable—we are having a dry spring, for once—and she left no tracks. But she rode into the

Bigelows' farm ten miles west of here and made off with two of his horses! The dogs set up a clamor, and Mr. Bigelow pursued her and after a long chase managed to capture her when her horse stepped into a hole. He told us when he brought her back that she fought like a wildcat. That was five days ago. At this moment she appears so subdued, so calm, that I cannot believe she bit and scratched him, although he claims to have the marks to prove it.

Mama and Martha are quite beside themselves over this, but Grandfather says that we must forgive her and pray for her. So there is much prayer going on in our household, for patience for ourselves as much as anything. Frankly she does appear to be completely heathen and is unmoved by our efforts. She has forgotten that her own father's father, Elder John Parker, actually founded a church in Illinois and brought it here to Texas, that had it not been for Elder John and his faith, she would not be here at all.

At least it was not while I was watching her that she ran away. Papa fell asleep when it was his turn to guard her through the night!

Two days ago a Mr. A. F. Corning arrived from Fort Worth with his camera. He had heard about Cynthia Ann—our cousin is very famous in these parts now, the Rescued Captive—and wanted to make a photograph of her. I tried to explain to her what was happening, but how does one go about explaining such a thing?

At any rate, she sat on a bench (*not* on the buffalo robe!), and while Mr. Corning was preparing to make his portrait, Topsannah crawled up on Cynthia Ann's lap to nurse. Cynthia Ann obligingly opened her shirtwaist and the child began to suck. Mama has not been able to persuade Cynthia Ann that she should not nurse the child in public; in this matter she is truly like an animal and thinks nothing of baring her breast, no matter who is present. "She is hungry," Cynthia Ann said, and we were so pleased at her English that we could not be displeased by her behavior.

Mama felt that this was not a fit subject for a photograph, but Mr. Corning seemed quite charmed by the maternal scene and captured it, despite my mother's protests. Mama announced that this so-called portrait will not be displayed in our home, but Grandfather has suggested that it be framed so that only Cynthia Ann's head and shoulders may be seen.

On top of all this, there is even more excitement. Cynthia Ann has been invited to journey to Austin next month to a meeting of the legislature, where she will be recognized by the State of Texas as the most famous of the captive women. We plan to accompany her, and since I have never traveled so far from home, I am in a fever of anticipation.

Mrs. Richard Bigelow—the one whose horses were stolen—and Mrs. Nathaniel Raymond and Mrs. John Henry Brown, all Birdville neighbors, have begun to come by each day to help get her ready. They are making her a handsome cloak of lightweight gray wool trimmed in black soutache and a blue and white silk dress with a pretty white collar. Mrs. Raymond has promised to lend Cynthia Ann a handsome silver brooch to complete the costume. It is quite a sociable atmosphere here at our cabin as the women gather to prepare Cynthia Ann for this great occasion.

Does she grasp what is happening? I think not. Her mind is so unlike ours. And her sadness seems as deep today as it did when she first came to us two months ago. It seems very odd to me that at one moment Cynthia Ann is trying to run away and we are all occupied in trying to bring her back and keep her here, and the next she is to be honored by our government.

Grandfather has come up with a fine idea. He has promised Cynthia Ann that if she does her best to learn the language and ways of the white man, she will be allowed to visit her Indian people again. He explained this to her slowly and carefully, and I could see in her eyes that she understood him. That very hour she came and sat beside me—drew up a stool, not her buffalo robe—and said quite plainly, "I learn to speak your way now."

So naturally we are pleased about this, although Mama does not entirely trust her, and Ben insists it is "another Indian trick." I must admit that they—and Jedediah and, of course, Martha—may be right. Only Grandfather and I truly believe in her, it seems.

Part II

SINTY-ANN

CHAPTER TEN

*T*he neighbor women tried to
explain it to her, but she had
no idea where they were going, or why. Could it be they were
taking her back to her People? She dared not hope too much.

After they had caught her the last time she had tried to
run away, White Hair told her that she could go back to the
People—she believed she had understood this—if she would
do certain things: she must learn the speech of white people,
and she must learn their ways.

She had thought this over and believed she could do what
he wanted, if it meant that she could go home. "For a visit,"
White Hair said. But once she was with the People again, there
would be no question of leaving to come back here. He would
see that, and he would not force her. And if he did not
understand—no matter. The People would not let her go.

And so she agreed to his request. Instead of shutting out the white people's words, she listened carefully when they spoke. Especially Loo-see. This was her language in the other time, the time before the People. If she tried, she knew she would be able to remember it.

Slowly she began to recognize more of their words, and she could make some sense of the strings of sounds that flew at her in a rush. Tentatively she struggled to speak their words, beginning by calling them by their names: Uncle, Anna, Isaac, Ben, Martha, Lucy, Sarah, James. She even began to use their name for her: Sinty-ann. Only to herself was she still Naduah. But she would not call her daughter Tecks Ann. Instead, she called her Prairie Flower, the meaning of Topsannah.

When the neighbor women came and dressed her in the new clothes they had made her, she tried to tell them that she needed buckskin to make the right kind of clothes to wear on her journey back to the People. But she didn't have all the words to explain, and they paid no attention to her.

If one of their men would shoot a deer or an antelope and bring her the skin, she would know what to do. She would soak the buckskin in water and ashes and scrape the hair and flesh from it, and she would work it until it was soft and supple, a beautiful color like the yellow fat they made from cow's milk. She knew exactly how to cut the skin with a knife and to stitch the pieces together. She had no buffalo sinew for stitching, but maybe their thread would do, or she could cut narrow strips of buckskin. And she would decorate her dress with fringes and beads so that when she returned to her husband and the rest of the tribe they would see that she was still one of them, unchanged by white ways. When she thought about seeing them again, her heart felt as light as a bird.

But she realized when they set out in their wagons pulled by plodding horses that they were not traveling north and west toward the plains but were moving south along a broad, hard-packed trail. Her heart sank. They were not going home.

Several families were making the trip—the Brown family and the Raymond family as well as a number of Parkers—reminding her of the times the People moved their camp. But this was so different!

When the People moved, as they did very often, it was to be nearer the buffalo or the white settlements they planned to raid or to find a sheltered place for the winter. The chief and a council of elders of the tribe decided when and where to move. Scouts chose the site, looking for a place with plenty of water and forage for the horses.

It was up to the women to make the preparations. They owned nothing that could not be easily moved; the less you had to carry with you, the better. Everything was packed in tanned hides, the sleeping skins rolled up, the tipi covers taken down from the lodgepoles, the poles pulled up and fastened to the saddles of horses and mules to drag the loads. Young children were tied to saddles on gentle mares or carried in cradleboards on their mothers' backs, the old and feeble rested on drags behind a reliable animal, and everyone else rode a favorite horse.

They traveled steadily, a long line of horses and people strung out across the prairie, until they had reached the site of the next camp. The women scrambled for position, choosing places in a rough circle around the chief's lodge. As Peta Nocona's wife, Naduah always had a choice spot.

Making a new place to live was as quick and simple as leaving the old one. The women helped each other put up the tipis, standing on one another's shoulders to fasten together the tops of the lodgepoles and to tie on the skins. A fire pit was dug, a fire built, cooking begun.

But these white people! It took days of preparation, packing their clothing in leather-covered wooden boxes that were loaded on the wagons, everything cumbersome and difficult. Sinty-ann rode stoically next to Uncle, Prairie Flower sitting on her lap.

She understood that Uncle was a brother of her father in the time before the People, and that father was now dead. "Killed by those same Indians that kidnapped you and John," Uncle said. She would not think about that. The mother, the one she remembered bathing her, the one who baked bread, was also dead. Uncle told her she had a sister and brother somewhere to the east. Not John, but another one, named Silas. "John stayed with the Indians," Uncle said. "We hear he married another captive, a little Mexican gal." That was all he would say. She could scarcely remember John or when he had disappeared.

When they first set out on the journey, everyone was in high spirits, talking and laughing. The sun shone, the breeze was fresh, and all around them little blue flowers bloomed on the rolling green fields.

"Austin," she heard them say often, and she thought that must be the name of a person. Later she realized Austin was the name of the place they were going. But what was to happen there? Why were they making this trip? She had no idea.

She heard talk, too, of "secession" and "legislature," but these words were meaningless to Sinty-ann.

When darkness came they stopped. Two dark-skinned slaves who traveled with them—Negroes, Uncle called them—set up the camp, carried water from a stream, and built a big fire. Why did white men enjoy such large fires while the People made only small ones that could not be seen so easily? The dark men also stood guard while the others slept. At daybreak they continued on their way.

After several days of travel, which tired everyone, they arrived in Austin. Sinty-ann had never before been in a settlement this large. Fort Worth, a half day's journey from Uncle's farm, was the biggest settlement she had ever seen; she had traveled there once with Uncle and Isaac to buy salt, sugar, and coffee. They called Fort Worth with its muddy central square a town. They called this Austin place a city, "the capital."

They found accommodations for the entire group in a large cabin with many rooms, some above the others, with steps leading up. A boardinghouse, they called it. Sinty-ann was given a room to share with Lucy and the young children and Mrs. Raymond and her two daughters. Lucy and Mrs. Raymond and one daughter took the big wooden bed with its snowy white cover. The children slept in a smaller bed pulled from under the big one, tumbled together like fox kits in a den. Sinty-ann spread her buffalo robe on the floor for herself and Prairie Flower. Ben had stayed behind with the other slaves to protect the farm, and no one seemed to be guarding her. They must have known she would be too frightened of this place to flee.

After they had had a day to rest themselves, the women dressed Sinty-ann in the blue and white dress with the white collar and Mrs. Raymond's silver brooch. She was still uncomfortable in these awkward clothes, but she knew that the women meant kindly and did not complain.

Then all but Prairie Flower and the youngest children, who stayed behind with the Negroes, set out together in horse-drawn carriages, which Uncle had hired. The carriages trotted smartly up a road leading to an enormous white building and rolled past a wide expanse of grass. They came to a stop at the broad steps that lead to the entrance with a row of tall, white pillars as thick as trees set across the front. Sinty-ann stared.

"It's the Texas State Capitol," one of the women said in a voice that trilled with excitement. "Isn't it grand?"

They walked into a great hall filled with white men who sat in rows listening while other white men spoke. Quietly the visitors took seats near the back, except for Uncle—dressed, Sinty-ann noted, in his finest suit and a black silk necktie. He strode briskly to the front of the hall, where he was greeted as a friend, and spoke privately to one of the men seated at a long table. Some of the men turned around to stare, and a murmur swept through the huge room.

Sinty-ann watched uneasily. Who were these men? When men gathered like this in the chief's lodge, it was to discuss matters that concerned the tribe and to make important decisions. Now one of the white chiefs at the table at the front of the hall rose and began to speak. She heard her name, and her apprehension turned to fear.

Mrs. Brown and Mrs. Raymond rose and pushed her forward. Uncle was striding toward her, his mouth smiling. She knew that everyone was staring, watching her. Were these white war chiefs, then? Were they going to decide her fate? Is that why she had been dressed up and brought all this long distance, to face these judges?

She looked around wildly, wanting to flee, not knowing which way to go. In a panic she broke away from the women who were leading her to the chiefs and tried to run from them. Maybe they would kill her as she ran. She didn't care; they could kill her if they wished.

But Mrs. Brown seized one arm and Mrs. Raymond the other, and she heard their hushed whispers trying to calm her. She was stronger than both of them, they were no match for her, but in a moment Uncle was beside her with Mr. Brown. She knew that she could not fight off all of them. She quit struggling and stood still, head down and eyes closed, waiting to learn her destiny.

Lucy explained it to her afterward. "They were honoring you, Sinty-ann. Everyone cares very much for you," she said, taking Sinty-ann's hand in hers. "They're giving you a league of land, for you and Prairie Flower to live on, if you want to. And they've promised to give you a hundred dollars every year. That's a lot of money. You can use it to buy things—you know, to trade. It's wonderful news, Sinty-ann! You should be pleased, not frightened. They are doing something good for you."

Sinty-ann understood some parts of what Lucy was telling

her. But it made no sense, the thing the men had decided to do. Why would they want to give her these gifts? And so she asked, "Why?"

"They want to make up to you for what you suffered all those years before you came to us," Lucy said.

It still made no sense, but she pretended that she understood and nodded her head.

After that, the white people would not leave her in peace. People kept coming to the boardinghouse to look at her, to ask her questions, or to talk to Uncle about her. They brought a large piece of paper with printing on it and showed her her picture. They called it a newspaper, but she didn't understand how that picture got there.

She also had to visit some of their homes, escorted by a member of the Parker family. A few of them even boldly asked her about her husband and her sons, not caring that the mention of them cut her like knives! They would not let her return to the People unless she promised to speak their language and live as they did, and yet they wanted to stare at her, to pry into her heart. And they fussed over her little girl, calling her Tecks Ann, picking her up and carrying her around, showing her off.

Prairie Flower seemed to like the attention. She laughed and chattered to these strangers, using the few white man's words that she had been taught. Sinty-ann longed to snatch the child from them, to hide her away so that they couldn't see her and she couldn't see or hear them. They acted as though the little girl belonged to them.

"Little heathen," she heard the women say when they had climbed into the wagons and started the long, tiring journey back to the farm. "We must do something about that."

"Scriptures, that's the thing," Mrs. Brown said to Anna. "I believe if you start teaching these poor lost souls the Word of God, it will make all the difference in the world to them."

"Yes, Ruth," Anna said. "We have been praying with them, but I agree that spending more time with the Good Book might be just the thing. Surely they can be taught to memorize some simple verses."

The women's conversation drifted past Sinty-ann's ears. She paid no attention to it. Maybe, she thought, when this long trip was over, Uncle would see how well she was taking on the ways of his people, and he would keep his promise to help her find her People.

In the wagon ahead of theirs, Lucy's yellow hair drifted lightly over the shawl she wore wrapped around her shoulders. Sinty-ann tried to imagine Lucy as one of the People, as she had been at that age, and the thought almost made her smile.

An idea came to her. Perhaps she could take Lucy with her when she went back. Not as a captive—she would ask Peta Nocona to see that she was not harmed, that she would be safely returned to her family (Sinty-ann could imagine Hair Beneath His Nose coming after them, shooting his gun, killing everyone in sight, as he had done at the attack on their camp). Then Lucy would understand, and she would be able to explain to Anna and Uncle and the others why Sinty-ann must remain there with her People, and not here with strangers who claimed to be her family.

But then she discarded that idea. Lucy's parents would never allow such a thing. Besides, Lucy might not be able to survive such a trip. She was a white girl, after all, not strong, not like the People. Not like her.

CHAPTER ELEVEN

From Lucy's journal, May 15, 1861

*I*t pleases me to write that Cynthia Ann seems truly to be keeping her promise to return to our language and customs. Grandfather's bargain that she can go back to her tribe for a visit if she does these things must have brought about this change. We can see that she is trying very hard and with great success.

She is less cooperative about Prairie Flower, though, believing, I suppose, that it is important for the child to learn Comanche ways. She may be right (no one else here would agree with me), because although the little girl is quite pretty, she does look Indian, and Mama says she may not be accepted by white society. Nevertheless, I do concede that we cannot let her continue in her heathenish ways, no matter whether she looks Indian or white.

Nearly every day now Mrs. Bigelow or Mrs. Brown or Mrs. Raymond comes by to drill the two of them in their Bible verses. Prairie Flower is only beginning to talk, but she sits obediently by her mother's side while Cynthia Ann repeats the verses, mimicking the ladies. They are working on the Beatitudes—"the Blesseds," as Papa calls them. I especially think of Cynthia Ann when I hear the second one, "Blessed are they that mourn: for they shall be comforted," for I am sure the poor thing does still mourn for her husband and sons. I am not certain she understands the words they want her to repeat over and over until she can say them from memory, but Mama insists that just *saying* the words is good for her and will soften her heart.

What I do not have the courage to tell Cynthia Ann is that no matter how many Bible verses she learns, she may not be able to visit her people for some time. We have learned that we are now engaged in a civil war, the South against the North. It was Jedediah who brought the news.

As Grandfather has explained it, when we were in Austin, Texas voted to join the other Southern states to form the Confederacy and has seceded from the Union. Jedediah has warned us that federal troops have been withdrawn from Fort Cooper as well as other frontier forts, and there is no one left to help fight the Indians. We are on our own now and, he says, in great danger. Also according to Jed, fighting has already begun in South Carolina, at the entrance to Charleston Harbor.

Martha spends much time weeping, for although Jed has not said so, she is afraid that he will go off to fight. We all pray that this war will end quickly.

CHAPTER TWELVE

*S*inty-ann rose from her buffalo robe spread on the cabin floor, and, to humor Anna, poured water from a pitcher into a basin kept out on the gallery, washed her face and hands with a bit of soap, and dried them on a clean blue cloth. This was the kind of thing that seemed so important to this white family and meant nothing at all to her.

The People rarely bathed, although after her monthly period a woman always immersed herself in a river or creek to take away her uncleanness, even in the winter when the water was frozen over and she had to break through the ice. Strangely, this was not something these white women did. They seemed to have no customs regarding their women's blood.

A woman of the People stayed in a separate tipi during those times, away from the men. That made sense: a woman's blood could take away a man's power, his medicine. When she was in her period, she was not permitted to carry her husband's shield or to go anywhere near him until she had bathed. Here, no one seemed to pay attention to such matters.

For instance, the boy, Ben, still lived in the house with the rest of the family. A boy like him would have moved into his own separate tipi long ago, to keep him away from the grease of the cooking pots, which everyone knew could contaminate him and was dangerous to his power. And this Ben spent far too much time around Martha and Lucy. No boy of the People would have been allowed anywhere near his sisters, would not have been permitted to touch them or even to speak to them. It seemed very odd to Sinty-ann—things that were important to the People had no importance to these white people, and the other way around.

Now that the white people's speech was coming back to her, she sometimes talked about such things with Lucy. Lucy was curious; she seemed to want to know about the People. At first Sinty-ann did not want to talk to her, afraid she would be like the others, despising the ways of the People. She had heard Uncle and Lucy's parents and brother Ben talking about the People, about Sinty-ann's husband and sons and family and friends. Although she did not always understand their words, she certainly understood their tone when they spoke with voices that rung with hatred, harsh laughter, and lack of respect.

But Lucy, although young, was different from the others in her family. She was of an age to be Sinty-ann's daughter, yet she seemed truly interested in Sinty-ann's life, her experiences. One day the women built a big fire in the yard and set over it a huge iron kettle of cooking grease and lard they had been saving up in buckets. When the fat had been melted and strained until it was clear, they stirred in liquid, water that had been allowed to drip through a trough full of wood ashes. Lye, Lucy called it.

For hours they took turns cooking and stirring the mess, until it turned white and creamy. Then they poured this into a box to cool and harden, and later they cut it into chunks. They called it soap and used it to wash their clothes and their own bodies. Such a lot of work to make this useless thing!

"And you had nothing like this?" Lucy asked, her blue eyes wide.

"No. Nothing."

"But how did you wash?"

"No washing. Not important to wash."

"But how did you get yourself clean?"

"Clean? What is clean?"

"It means not dirty."

Sinty-ann thought about it. "Clean, dirty, no difference. Not important."

After a while Lucy stopped asking about washing and cleanliness and turned to a new subject. "What about cooking? How did you cook?"

"Put meat close to fire and it cooks. Sometimes we put meat in a pot. When I was young like you, no pot. Traders did not bring pots, so we cook in skins, in buffalo's belly. But if skins are too close to fire, they burn up! So we put meat and water in buffalo's belly and drop hot stones from fire into meat and water. Stones make water hot and cook meat. Simple."

Lucy always smiled and shook her head when Sinty-ann explained things that way: *simple*.

"And was that all you ate? Just buffalo?"

"Mostly buffalo. We kill him and dry meat, make jerky. We dry fruit and pound it, and pound jerky, mix with other things. Pemmican, we call it. All winter, when nothing else comes, we eat jerky and pemmican. Also eat antelope and deer, not as good as buffalo. When animals go someplace else, we look for other things to eat. That is work of women, to gather food."

"What kinds of things did you gather?"

She shrugged. She did not know the names of the nuts they collected or the wild fruits they picked and dried, using the seeds of some of them to form a paste that could be stored for the hungry times. "Nothing like you eat," she said. "I dig things from earth, I grind seeds and mix with what comes from bones of buffalo. Other thing we like is honey. Like you."

It always seemed to please Lucy when Sinty-ann could find something similar in their lives, like honey. But not much was.

"But you didn't have a garden," Lucy would say, almost sadly.

"No garden," Sinty-ann agreed. How could she explain how foolish it seemed to her to spend so much time digging and planting and waiting for things to grow when you could go out and find food wherever you happened to be?

"And what about fish?" Lucy's hands made a swimming motion. "We really enjoy good fish right out of the creek."

Sinty-ann shook her head. "No fish. Bad to eat fish. Bad to eat chickens. And big bird like a chicken, very bad."

"Big bird?" Lucy wondered. "You mean the turkey?"

"Yes, turkey. Men eat turkey and become cowards and run away from their enemy."

"And you don't like pork. Meat from the pig."

"No pig."

"But that's mostly the kind of meat we eat," Lucy said. "They're so easy to raise. And we can preserve the meat by smoking. I think it's a lot easier than making jerky."

"Pig lives in mud and water," Sinty-ann said firmly. "My People do not eat animals that live in mud and water. Not good."

"And you actually ate the buffalo's liver raw?" Lucy asked, shuddering. "It makes me sick to think of it."

"Very good," Sinty-ann told her. "You don't like it because you are not Nermernuh."

"Nermernuh?"

"Our word for the People."

"Not Comanche? You don't call yourselves Comanches?"

"White man call us Comanche. They learn it from other Indians, our enemies. Not our word. I am Nerm," she said proudly. "We are Nermernuh."

Later she heard Lucy explaining this to Isaac and Anna and Ben and Martha.

"Doesn't matter much what she calls them, does it?" Ben asked angrily. "They're still just dirty Indians."

Lucy hushed him. "She'll hear you! She understands!"

It was true. She understood more and more.

These conversations about her life with the People had a mixed effect on Sinty-ann. The memories they brought back were both pleasant and painful. It seemed that she would not be going to see the People now because something had happened, a battle among white men, that prevented Uncle from keeping his promise. When she talked to Lucy about the People, it helped her not to forget.

But she would say nothing about Peta Nocona. Lucy asked shyly, "Will you tell me about your husband? About Peta Nocona? What was he like? Was he good to you?"

"I do not speak of him," Sinty-ann said.

"I'm sorry," Lucy said hurriedly. "I wasn't trying to pry. I was just curious."

"I do not speak of him."

Their lessons had become more formal. Lucy wanted her to learn the names of the months and the days of the week. Sinty-ann had never thought of time being divided up like this, or if she had once known it, she had forgotten.

"When I came here?" Sinty-ann asked.

"January," Lucy said. "But Captain Ross and the other Rangers found you last December. Around Christmastide."

"And now?" Sinty-ann asked. "What is it now?"

"July. You've been here with us for six months. Half a year."

Year? That had to be explained, too, along with how many days there were in each month. To help her remember, Lucy taught her a little spoken song, a poem: "Thirty days hath September, April, June, and November. . . ."

But before any of this made sense, she had to learn numbers and counting. Lucy showed her how to use her fingers, and then showed her signs on paper that stood for numbers.

Next Lucy wanted her to learn to read a clock. She called it "telling time." This seemed pointless to Sinty-ann. Why did anyone need numbers for this? Surely you knew when the sky was brightening before sunrise, and you could watch as the sun moved across the sky, and you could see when it was setting and when night had come. What else did anyone need?

She paid little attention to the lessons on the clock that Uncle wound each night with a key or to the name of each day. This was important to the white people in order to remember a day they called the Sabbath. On that day the men did not work in the fields, the women did less work, and the children were not allowed to play. Instead they prayed together and read from a big book. Was it not enough to watch the moon, to see what the earth produced in each season, to feel the change from cold to warm? But Lucy kept trying.

"Next I'm going to teach you to read," Lucy said determinedly. "Then you'll be able to read our Bible. I can teach you to write, too. And when Prairie Flower is old enough, I'll teach *her*."

Sinty-ann smiled at that. What would Peta Nocona say when he learned that his wife could read the white man's writing? And write it, too?

CHAPTER THIRTEEN

From Lucy's journal, August 8, 1861

Oh, how bitter this is! If something has happened to Cynthia Ann, I can blame only myself, and I am certain everyone else is already blaming me. I am so ashamed at the trouble I have caused, and now there is nothing for me to do but pray.

It all began quite calmly. Every evening, when the sun has set and the air is a little cooler, Cynthia Ann and I have fallen into the habit of walking to my sister's new cabin to see what progress has been made. This has become a time for us to talk together, when there is no chance of anyone overhearing us. What began as "English lessons" has now become real conversation, as Cynthia Ann's mind again grasps the language of her childhood. She speaks in a rather odd, flat accent and her sentences are stiff, like an unused muscle. But the words are mostly there, and they seem to emerge more and more easily.

I am quite comfortable with her, and I believe she is with me. Or was. I had even begun to feel that she trusted me.

Yesterday, I shall always remember, Cynthia Ann described exactly how a tipi is made. She insists that the tipis she lived in were much better than our log cabins! "This door does not look toward east," she remarked when she saw the little cabin growing up out of the ground as Papa and Jedediah and Ben, still a help with only one arm, laid each squared-off log in place. "Uncle's door does not look toward east."

Martha, who had come out of her half-finished cabin to greet us, seemed angry at this. "Why, pray tell, do you think they should face east?" she asked.

"All doors must look to where the sun rises."

"Why is that important?" I wanted to know.

"When they wake up, men leave their lodge and bow to the rising sun. Warriors smoke pipes and blow smoke to east."

At that, Martha simply shook her head and walked away, not bothering to explain that we build our cabins facing south in order to catch the breezes that blow in from that direction in summer. And I was more interested in hearing Cynthia Ann's explanation.

"But *why*, Cynthia Ann?"

I am truly curious about her Indian beliefs, how the sun is the source of all living things, and the earth is the mother, and the moon and stars are somehow important, too. I knew that Mama and Papa would not approve of our talking about these pagan ideas, and I was glad that Martha was not there to hear. So I continued to ask questions, and Cynthia Ann answered as best she could.

If they heard her, this would disappoint my parents and Grandfather, who believe that she is giving up her heathen ideas. She might recite the 23rd Psalm word for word when Grandfather asks her to, but when she says "The Lord is my shepherd, I shall not want," it is not our God she is thinking about. It is the Great Spirit, or the sun, or the buffalo, or some such. I hold my tongue and do not tell her that her pagan ideas are sinful, because she seems so innocent! She's like a child, even though I am sure she is as old as Mama! And I shall further hold my tongue and not tell any of my family of our talks about religion, because that would upset them. Grandfather is convinced that Cynthia Ann is forgetting her godless beliefs and is becoming again the Christian she was born. It is not for me to tell him that he is mistaken.

Every evening we gather at the table and Grandfather leads us in prayer, never failing to ask special blessings for Cynthia Ann and Tecks Ann (as he still calls her), calling upon the Lord to open their hearts and to cleanse them of their sinfulness. But what sinfulness? Was living among her people really a sin? I cannot ask these questions, because in their eyes I am too young, although I am now two months past my thirteenth birthday, and must not ever think such thoughts.

Cynthia Ann still will not speak to me about her husband, no matter how cleverly I have tried to draw her out on this subject. Sometimes she says, "I do not speak of him." Other times she pretends not to hear or understand, her lips firmly closed, the muscles of her jaw quite rigid.

Sometimes she does speak of her children, if I ask the questions just right. "They will be great warriors," she has told me several times, and it is useless to try to convince her that being a warrior is not a good thing, that they will surely be killed if they become warriors.

"That is very dangerous," I say carefully. "I certainly wouldn't want my brother, Ben, to be a warrior, even though he can handle a gun as well as any man. He'll be a farmer, like our father."

She looks at me as though I am not right in the head. "Yes, dangerous. But it is what a man of Nermernuh does. Many men die in battle."

And last evening I tried again to persuade her on this subject. "But your men don't have to die that way, Cynthia Ann," I said. "They must give up their raids on the farms of white settlers. They must stop stealing horses and killing people and taking scalps. It's *wrong*, you know. The Bible says—"

"*You* say wrong," she said, cutting me short. "Your Bible says wrong. What does that mean to us? We are Nermernuh, and that is our way, Lucy. Other is *your* way, white man's way. We are not like you. I think you forget that."

"But you're white!" I said. "How can you believe those things?"

"You say I am white. I say I am Nerm."

I knew it was wrong to argue, but I found myself getting riled. And then I said something quite unforgivable.

"How can you believe that, Cynthia Ann? Those Nermernuh that you love so much *killed most of your family!* And they kidnapped you and your brother and other people, too! Surely you remember that? And what about what happened to you after they captured you? If you remembered what they did to you and your family, I do not think you would love them so much, even if you did marry one!"

Cynthia Ann stared at me for a moment, her eyes filled with anger and confusion and sadness, and then she turned and walked away—not back toward our cabin, but away from the farm and into the woods. Naturally I was upset that such a bad feeling had come between us, and I instantly regretted not holding my tongue. But I thought it was just a temporary thing, that she needed to compose herself and then I would apologize and we would go on as before. Besides, Prairie Flower was with me. The little Indian child was humming contentedly to herself, playing in a pile of sawdust next to the cabin that would be my sister's new home, seeming not even to notice that her mother had left.

But then darkness began to fall, and I realized that Cynthia Ann had disappeared, deep into the wilderness. I could not go in after her, not with Prairie Flower. By the time I returned to our cabin with the child—who was by then upset by the disappearance of her mother—it was quite dark. They wanted me to tell them what had happened, but I could not bring myself to confess at that moment all that I had said that had led up to her flight. Especially since Mama is coming close to her time, and I do try hard not to trouble her. So I said only, "She got upset and she went into the woods."

They were content to let this go and did not press me for details, believing that she would soon come back on her own. They believed, as I did, that she would not try to run away without a horse, that she would never try to go back to her people without her child, and that in a matter of a few hours she would forget her anger and come home.

But the night wore on, and there was no sign of her. Grandfather had gone to Dallas on business, or I am certain that he would have plunged into the woods without any hesitation, but Papa and Ben were not so anxious. And I knew that I could not do it alone.

"She'll be back when she gets hungry enough," Mama kept saying in a sour tone. She is heavy with the child and tires easily, and her patience is worn thin.

I forgot about that when I cried, "But what if something happened to her! Suppose animals got her. Or she's hurt and cannot come back. Oh, we must go find her!"

"She can take care of herself well enough, Lucy," Mama assured me in a gentler tone. "She'll be back when she's ready. I wouldn't worry myself too much about it."

But I did worry, and all of today I have done little else but wait and pray to Almighty God for her return.

Then late this afternoon when I went out to the privy and was once more searching the distance for her, I happened to look off to the north and saw a thin dark line of clouds stretching across the sky, the first sign of a blue norther coming our way. By the time I had hurried back to the cabin, the air had taken on an eerie stillness. Papa and Ben rushed in from the fields, calling to us to get the animals shut up as best we could and the shutters latched.

In minutes the dark line became an ominous wall of black thunderclouds, and the wind began to blow, bending the trees. When the rains began in lashing sheets, I was beside myself with worry. What shelter will she find out there in the woods?

Papa says not to fret, that she is well able to take care of herself, but as the wind howls and the hail drums on the roof of our cabin, I cannot imagine how she will endure this. And Prairie Flower weeps in fear of the storm and in despair that her mother is not here.

I know that Mama would be relieved to be rid of her, and Martha and Ben and Papa, too. It is only Grandfather and I who truly care for her. But for the sake of the little girl, I am desperate for her return. I have resolved that if she does not return soon, I will take a horse and go looking for her myself. And pray that I find her alive.

CHAPTER FOURTEEN

*T*he hot, moist air hung motionless, and the white women's
clothing clung to Sinty-ann's legs, heavy and clammy. Insects
hummed and bit, raising small, red-and-white, itching welts
on her hands and face.

Lucy had made her very angry. In some ways Sinty-ann
had grown fond of the girl. Lucy was kind, and she meant no
harm. She was the only one in this family who seemed to try
to understand, who did not despise the People. And yet even
Lucy had shown that she was capable of cruelty, without even
knowing that she was being cruel.

The questions Lucy had flung at her had hit their mark,
upsetting her deeply. In all the time Sinty-ann had lived with
the People—"Twenty-five years," Lucy had said, "since you

were like Sarah"—she had chosen not to think about how she came to be there with them. She knew terrible things had happened then, things that must be forgotten. But as she grew older, the memories had sunk like stones in water, out of reach, far below the surface, rising up again only in dreams. Then, even the dreams had stopped.

But since she had been forced to live among these white people, the dreams had come back, waking her in the night, her sleeping gown soaked with sweat, her moans disturbing Prairie Flower. It is nothing, she told herself—only a dream. When it happened many times, she knew that it was more than that.

Then Lucy spoke of those forgotten things as though she knew about the dreams. Somehow Lucy knew what had happened—but how *could* she know? Lucy had not yet been born in the time before Sinty-ann was Naduah.

The sun slipped over the edge of the world, and darkness moved in swiftly. Sinty-ann pushed through the thick growth until she could no longer see the branches that snapped at her face. Then she threw herself on the mossy ground and lay stretched out, feeling the damp earth along the length of her body. The sounds of the woods were changed. She listened to the owl calling, over and over. Her stomach began to gnaw with hunger, and she was thirsty. The night passed slowly. She gathered a few leaves and sucked the droplets of moisture that had collected on them, but it was not enough to slake her thirst. She lay still, making no effort to move.

She believed they would not come looking for her yet, because they thought she would not go far—not without Prairie Flower. They were right. She would not try to make her way back to the People this time. All she wanted now was to get away from that white family. All of them, even Lucy.

The light returned, and the heat. Her hunger and thirst deepened. Late in the day, she felt the change in the air. Everything became very still. Then the wind began to blow. She knew what this meant: a violent storm, the kind that sometimes swept across the prairies and tore all but the most firmly pegged tipis out of the ground and blew them away, whipping them with driving rains that stripped the leaves from the trees. She looked around for shelter, but there was none. At least, she thought grimly, as the force of the storm broke, they would not come for her in this. Neither would wild animals.

She huddled against a tree, listening to the wind that howled like a wounded beast. Now there was water to drink, but she was shivering with cold. Sometime later the storm passed on. She squeezed the water out of her sodden clothes and drank it. Then it was night again.

She thought of her sons, remembering when they had gone on their vision quests, seeking their power, their medicine.

The vision quest was an experience every young brave went through. When he was no longer a boy but not yet a man, he left the camp dressed in his breechcloth and moccasins, carrying only his buffalo robe, a pipe, some tobacco, and a flint or a bit of metal for starting a fire. He went alone. That night he slept facing east, his robe over his head, showing that he was not afraid of wild animals that might attack him in the darkness. For four days and nights, longer if necessary, he fasted and prayed, waiting for his vision, trusting that some spirit would share its power with him.

Sometimes the spirit came to the youth as a voice heard in a trance, or as an animal that appeared to him, giving him songs to chant whenever he wanted to make medicine. *Puha*, it was called—power. That vision, that hallucination, gave him his medicine, telling him what to put in his medicine pouch—feathers, maybe, or the teeth or fur of a particular animal—so that he could contact his spirit when he needed to. It made him strong in battle, successful on hunts. No chief, no leader of the People, could be without medicine. If he did not have it, no warriors would follow him on a war party or go with him to hunt buffalo.

She remembered Quanah's vision quest. When he came back, it was clear that Quanah had powerful medicine. From the very beginning, even as a youth scarcely beyond boyhood, she knew, her husband knew, everyone knew, that Quanah would be a great leader.

For Pecos, the younger brother, it had not been that way. He had gone on his quest and come back without *puha*. They went to the medicine man for help, asking him for some of his *puha* for Pecos, but even that had not helped much. Several times Pecos went on a quest, and several times he returned, his discouragement deepening.

She had not loved him less for it, but she knew her husband was disappointed. This younger son would never lead a war party. But Quanah would, and that made up for everything.

Most of the old men in the tribe had *puha*. Even some of the women got it, but only after they were no longer able to bear children. Then their husbands would help them to get medicine.

Her husband was not here to help her get *puha*. But Naduah would get something else, alone here in the woods with her hunger and cold. She would remember what she had forgotten, and that would make her strong.

On the evening of the third day, leaning weakly against a tree trunk, she finally recalled the sound of her father's voice. It released a flood of memory that poured through her like a powerful river.

IT IS WARM, smelling of late spring. Her father and the other men come back from working in the fields, their blue shirts dark with sweat. She is helping her mother carry their supper to a rough wooden table outside the cabin. Her younger brother, John, and the two little ones, Silas Junior and Orlena, are still playing. She is tired of chasing them all day, glad when her father scoops them up on his lap and laughs with them, glad when they finally are tucked in their bed and she can stay up a while longer with the grown-ups and listen to their talk.

Her grandfather, Elder John Parker, and grandmother and her two uncles and their families as well as her own all live in the fort they have built, seven small cabins inside the stockade. Her cabin is next to the garden in which this summer's corn, beans, and peas are already sprouting. There are always lots of children to play with. They have lived in the fort for a couple of years. Before that there was the endless trip across the plains in wagons drawn by teams of oxen. Her youngest brother and little sister were born on that trip. Before that she lived in another place she can no longer remember at all.

The grown-ups' talk turns again to the Indians, especially the Comanches, who are constantly raiding the white settlements, stealing their horses, ruining their fields, sometimes killing the settlers. That was why the family had built this fort.

An enormous gate was made especially to keep the Indians out, put together without nails, made of wooden slabs so thick no bullet, no arrow shot from a powerful bow, could penetrate. Two blockhouses were erected at opposite corners of the compound where the men would go with their rifles in case of an attack. The surrounding stockade is made of logs twice as tall as any man, pointed at the top to keep Indians from climbing over.

The settlers feel secure inside their fort. "Indians won't never bother us here," her father says often when she feels scared. "We're safe, long as we keep that gate shut tight." A thrill of fear prickles her neck whenever the subject comes up.

Not long after dark, Elder John leads them in prayer, and the families drift to their own cabins. The great gate has been closed since the men came in from the fields. Everyone goes to bed; all is quiet save for the sound of the family's deep, even breathing. She drifts off to sleep, unafraid.

The next morning they are all up early, as usual.

Her uncles have already left for the fields where they will work all day. She watched them go out through the gate, left standing open to catch the fresh breezes. Her father is preparing to join them. She is washing the bowls and cups from their breakfast and keeping an eye on her baby sister for Mama when she hears her father shout: "Indians! Indians! There are hundreds of them headed this way!"

She peeps out and sees them, all those men on horses, fiercely painted, riding toward the stockade in a billowing cloud of dust. Fearfully she snatches up the baby and runs to find her mother.

In a moment there is confusion everywhere. And no one thinks to close the massive gate.

Cousin Sarah is already running out to the fields a mile away to warn the men. And then she sees her uncle Benjamin walking bravely out to speak to the Indians who are gathered menacingly just outside their fort.

Scarcely daring to breathe, she and her brother John cling to their mother. She can tell that her mother is frightened, too; she keeps whispering to her father, "Silas, what's going to happen? What are we going to do?"

"I don't know," he answers, his voice flat.

Benjamin comes back, white-faced. "They want beef," he explains shortly. "They also said they want water, although that don't make much sense, because they've just come from the river and their horses are still wet."

"What's their mood, brother?"

"They're carrying a white flag, they say they've come in peace. I don't trust them, but we have no choice." He begins to gather the food and water they have demanded.

Her father steps forward. "Benjamin, don't go."

"I have to," her uncle says, and he brushes Silas aside and goes to gather the supplies for the Indians.

The others watch, paralyzed with fear, as the youngest Parker brother strides out to meet the Comanches. "They're going to kill him," Silas says to her mother.

And then the killing begins.

The Indians, with chilling whoops and yells, immediately surround Benjamin and drive their spears into him. Cynthia Ann hides her face as they scalp him, cutting off a circle of skin and hair from the crown of his head and brandishing their trophy with more yells.

Then the Indians charge into the fort, pouring through the open gate. A few of them roughly seize her cousin Rachel, who clutches her baby, James, in her arms. Silas is suddenly galvanized into action and rushes to help the shrieking, struggling Rachel. Moments later Silas lies dead and Rachel and the baby are being dragged away.

"Come! Hurry, Cynthia Ann! John! Oh, hurry —hurry!" Her mother is screaming, sobbing, trying to drag the girl and her two brothers and the baby away from the howling Indians, toward the small rear gate. She sees her grandparents and Rachel's mother running that way, too.

But several Indians, their horses snorting and stomping, surround the five of them, and thrusting their bloody tomahawks in her mother's face, force her to let go of the girl. She is dragged away from her wailing mother and thrown on a horse behind a snarling, almost naked warrior. The man yells something, and she sees her brother John being seized and put on another horse. The captors wheel and dash out of the stockade. The dust is so thick she can scarcely see, but she does recognize her father's body and then her uncle Benjamin's as the horses gallop over them.

Blood is everywhere.

At first she is too terrified to cry out, to scream, to do anything. She looks back as her captor rides away from the fort and sees two warriors scalping the bodies of her father and her grandfather. Other Indians are running through the cabins, stealing and plundering, grabbing whatever weapons and ammunition they can find. Some of them are setting fire to the fields and outbuildings. In a frenzy of killing and destruction they slaughter some of the animals but leave others. What has happened to her mother and the others? There is no sign of them.

Then she sees the Indians rip open the feather mattresses from the beds with their spears. The last thing she sees is the feathers swirling through the air, thick as snow. She thinks about that afterward: it has been a long time since she last saw snow.

THE INDIANS AND THEIR CAPTIVES ride half the night. For a while she is too dazed to do anything. Her tongue is swollen with thirst, but she dozes a little, slumped against her captor's back. When they stop and make camp on the open prairie, someone ties her hands together behind her back, lashes her feet with leather thongs, and flings her onto the rough ground near the fire.

The Indians dance around them, yelling and shaking something in her face, something made from white hair. After a moment she realizes that it is her grandfather's scalp, and she turns her head away. One of the Indians strikes her with his wooden bow and forces her to look. They kick her and beat her. Once she catches a glimpse of her brother John, his eyes huge with fear and pain, and she hears the cries of Rachel's baby. After a while, the baby's cries grow weaker and then stop altogether. Is he dead, she wonders?

Throughout the long night the torment continues. Then for a time it is relatively quiet while the Indians rest, and she falls into an exhausted sleep.

At first light she is jerked awake again and thrust on a horse behind a warrior, but she is not certain if he is the same savage or a different one. She begs for food or at least something to drink, but he refuses and slaps her when she cries.

This is how it goes on day after day, night after night: a long, hard ride with nothing to eat and only enough to drink to allow her to survive, followed by a long night of abuse as the Comanches continue to celebrate their victory at Parker's Fort.

All that keeps her alive through those days is her concern for her brother John, six years old, his face and body swollen with purplish bruises. Mama always told her she must look out for him. Her own body looks much the same, and she knows that her face must also be distorted from the blows she has received. They are still alive—but who will ever come to save them?

And what has happened to Rachel and the baby, James? And to Aunt Elizabeth? They disappeared, and she does not know if they are dead or alive, or if they have simply been taken away. She looks around frantically for her brother to reassure herself that he is still here, that she is not entirely alone.

And then he is gone, too. The group has split and taken him away.

The terror does not end. She is a slave, she understands that. When she weeps in misery and loneliness for her mama and papa and the rest, they beat her. She learns to hide her tears, to present a stoic face.

After a time she is sent to live with some people

in the tribe, Speckled Eagle and his wives, Calls Louder and Walking At Night. She has to serve them, do whatever they demand. Speckled Eagle doesn't beat her, but the women do, slapping her and hitting her with a stick whenever she does something wrong, or she is too slow, or they feel like it. She has to work hard, carrying water, gathering wood, doing much harder work than the sons and daughters of Speckled Eagle and his wives. She learns not to complain, that it only makes things worse.

Time passes. Her wounds and bruises heal. She begins to understand what is being said to her. She learns to answer in their words. Her body grows taller and stronger. They begin to treat her better.

Then she becomes a woman and goes to stay in the tipi of the women who are in their period. She discovers that she likes being there with them.

It is soon after that time when the white traders come and try to speak to her. Their words sound strange. She can't think what to say to them. There are things she wants to ask, things she wants to say, but she is afraid—afraid of what they will do, afraid of what the People will do. Besides, something has begun to change inside her. She is no longer a terrified child. She is a woman. And no longer a slave, but one of the People. She has begun to find her place among the People. Gradually she stops thinking about the bad things that happened to her.

In the beginning she thought all the time about

running away. She made plans—that someday her chance would come, and she would go back to her home and her family. That is what the traders want her to do; she understands that.

But her home is destroyed; her family dead. She pictures again her father lying in a pool of blood, her uncle Benjamin with a spear through his chest, her grandfather's white scalp that was part of their dance those first horrible nights. She sees once more the terror on her mother's face. Surely they killed her mother, too, and the other children. And who knows what has become of John? She remembers the snow of feathers, drifting through the warm spring air, and confusion rises in her heart.

Where would she go then, with neither home nor family? She has no idea. What would these white traders do with her, where would they take her? Could they give her a better life than the one she has? The People have taken away her old life as cruelly as they took away her family. But they have also given her a new life. Hard as it is, she is afraid of losing what she has now. She knows that she cannot survive away from the People, so she says nothing, only stares at the ground. The traders go away.

The seasons pass, one after another. She marries. She bears children. She lives among the People, sharing their life. It becomes her life. The white drift of feathers comes to her only in dreams, swirling around the faces of her mama and papa and the others, like snowflakes.

The river of Sinty-ann's memory flowed strongly all through the night. She leaned against a tree trunk, eyes open and staring, seeing again the scenes of long ago in vivid clarity.

Then she saw something else: the golden eyes of a cat, all black except for those eyes, watching her from the limb of a tree. A panther, hunting for food. She knew this animal: if it was hungry, it would kill a human. She knew that this panther was not from her memory but from right now. But she was not afraid. This panther would not harm her. This was her *puha*, her power.

Shakily she got to her feet and spoke to the panther in the language of the People. She told him that she knew he had brought her medicine, and she thanked him. Then she turned her back on him and began to make her way slowly through the wilderness; the big cat gliding silently from branch to branch through the trees above her.

CHAPTER FIFTEEN

From Lucy's journal, August 10, 1861

I shall never forget last night as long as I live.

Cynthia Ann had been gone for three days. Mama and Ben believed that she had found a horse, perhaps a wild one, and was already far away. (It seems there is no horse she cannot ride, and astride, as men do, not sidesaddle.) Papa and Martha had another opinion, that she had been killed by some wild animal. Whichever way it was, Jedediah claimed we were well rid of her, and Grandfather was not yet back from Dallas to disagree and set things right.

But I knew in my heart that she was somewhere in the woods, in some hidden break or draw or thicket, able in her Indian way to endure the storm that stripped the pears from Mama's tree, and able to remain completely still and undetected while Papa and Ben and Jed might have passed within inches of her.

At last I could stand it no longer and determined to go in search of my cousin. I would take Prairie Flower with me, trusting that the sound of the little girl's voice would draw her mother out of hiding. But I dared not tell anyone my plan, especially Mama. Her time is nearly here for the birth of our new baby sister or brother, and she is nervous and rather delicate. Papa has not stayed out searching for Cynthia Ann as long as he might, saying that his place is with Mama. I cannot disagree—but whose place is with Cynthia Ann?

During the night I awoke to the sound of Prairie Flower's quiet sobs—she missed her mother dreadfully, partly, I suppose, because she is still nursing. Or was, until Mama gave her milk from our cow, Lulu, in a small cup. She took to that quite readily, but I think she misses the closeness of her mother.

And so I got up to soothe her, walking her to and fro to keep her sobs from waking the others. The nights now are very hot, and we have taken our pallets out on the gallery to sleep where there is a breeze. I stepped carefully over the sprawling figure of my brother Ben, and tiptoed past Sarah and James. I could make out Mama's rounded shape curled next to my father's long, skinny form.

Without much thought to what I was doing, I carried Prairie Flower across the yard and led Boots, Mama's gentle old bay with its two white stockings, quietly out of the shed. When we reached the edge of the clearing I set the sleepy Prairie Flower on Boots's back and used a fence rail to mount, and finally we were on our way.

There was not much of a moon, and what there was hung

so low in the sky that it offered scarcely any light. I gave Boots a free rein, since I did not have any plan as to where we would go, and let her pick her way through the thick, dark greenness however she wished.

I thought it would be difficult to get Prairie Flower awake and talking, but it was not. The child was born to be on a horse! She seemed delighted to wake up and find herself riding through the woods, and soon she was chattering merrily, as though this were the most ordinary thing in the world to do.

I had not had the presence of mind to fetch along any food or water, and soon Prairie Flower began to whimper. I myself grew weary as the night wore on, as well as hungry and thirsty. I began to realize how foolish I had been.

Never have I defied my parents and done that which they have strictly forbidden me to do. But what they did not know, they could not forbid, I told myself, knowing I would never have been given permission for this undertaking. I trusted Boots to find our way back, although I had no idea where we were, but I did not want to return without Cynthia Ann. And so we plodded on, forcing our way through the thick growth. Branches slapped at our faces. The darkness began to fade to a grayish light.

Presently Prairie Flower ceased whimpering and began to wail. We reached a small clearing and stopped to rest. I had begun to think we must turn back defeated when I made out a bedraggled figure stumbling toward us. Overjoyed, I prepared to call out, "Cynthia Ann! Here we are!" But the words stuck in my throat, for at that moment I saw, stalking silently behind her, a panther, black as Satan's heart. He seemed in no hurry to attack, taking his time.

Boots sensed the danger and stopped short, ears flattened back. For a moment we stared at each other, I at the panther, the panther at the horse, the child, and the foolish girl. Cynthia Ann kept on walking slowly toward us, unaware of the danger.

I am a fair shot. Papa saw to that, teaching all of us to handle a rifle as soon as we were big enough to hold one. Martha is excellent and before she met Jedediah liked to hunt squirrels and rabbits with Ben, who does quite well with his one good arm. They did not like to take me with them because I was "too young." But then Martha got to be "too old," I guess. She is much different now that she is about to become somebody's wife, and she no longer wants to go hunting with her brother. Martha could have dropped the panther easily. And so could I, but I had not thought to bring Papa's gun.

And then, from somewhere behind me, or off to the side, a rifle cracked, and the beautiful but deadly creature dropped in its tracks. I spun around and saw my brother Ben, sitting on his horse. He made no move to come to us, but I slid down from Boots and ran eagerly toward Cynthia Ann, pulling her little girl after me, happy to see her again and certain that she would be grateful that Ben had saved her life.

Instead, she turned her face away from me and covered it with her hands. Perhaps, I thought, she is distraught from her ordeal—tired, hungry, thirsty, tormented by insects. But she lowered her hands and stared at the dead animal. Then she turned to me with stark, haunted eyes. *"Puha,"* she said. "He did not mean to, Lucy, but he has killed my *puha*."

I did not understand, still do not, and had no idea what to say and so I said nothing. She was weak and trembling, and after a time she accepted my offer to ride back on Boots. It astounds me, the grace with which she can mount a horse, even when she is exhausted! And then I handed up to her the tired and grumpy Prairie Flower, who curled up in her mother's arms and promptly fell asleep.

When I turned around again, Ben was gone. Our small procession, Boots with her two riders and I, made its way back to the cabin. I was certain the worst for me was yet to come: facing Mama and Papa. But there was no chastisement; they were too busy to take much notice, for Mama's time had come.

As I write this, her labor pains have begun and Papa has ridden off to fetch Mrs. Bigelow to help. Martha is with her now, and she has told me, in that way my sister has now that she is about to be married, that I must stay with the children because I have, once again, behaved like one.

CHAPTER SIXTEEN

*Y*ou go," Sinty-ann said firmly. "I stay with your mama."

Martha glared at Sinty-ann. "I'm staying until Mrs. Bigelow gets here. That's who Mama wants to be with her. She doesn't want you, Sinty-ann. It's not your place." She sounded nervous and upset.

"Not *your* place," Sinty-ann replied calmly. "I have borne children; you have not. It is the place of mothers to help each other."

She could see that Martha didn't really want to be there with her mother. Anna Parker had been in labor since before sunrise; not long for a young, strong woman, but a long time for a woman Anna's age, the same as Sinty-ann's. Martha was frightened; she was not used to birthing. They had sent the wrong one away, Sinty-ann thought; young as she was, Lucy would not be nervous. If she was frightened, she would not show it. She would be calm and do whatever had to be done.

"It's all right," Anna said to Martha. "You go."

At last Martha left them alone, and Sinty-ann looked down at the woman in the bed. "You will have the baby here, in this cabin?" she asked.

"Certainly," Anna answered wearily. "Where would you have me go?" Her eyes were ringed with dark circles.

A Nerm woman did not have her baby in her tipi. Instead, she went to a hut that she had built of brush with a comfortable bed of moss. Two stakes were driven into the ground beside the bed to hold onto and a pit made for a small fire to heat water. There would have been a supply of sage to burn to purify the hut. There was just room enough inside for a couple of women to attend her. No men were allowed near, although if there were problems with the birth they sent for a medicine man. But Nerm women were strong, and usually all went well.

Sinty-ann pulled up a low stool and sat down beside the bed. There was nothing to be done for now; she could tell that the baby was not ready to be born just yet. Sinty-ann had had nothing to eat for several days; she was hungry and thirsty, as well as tired. But she would stay with Anna now, for Anna needed her.

She stayed by Anna's side, wondering if she dared to sing the doleful, monotonous songs that the women of the People always sang in the birthing huts. She guessed not. As in most everything, these white people had a different way of doing things, even having babies.

Suddenly things changed. She could tell by the difference

in the sounds Anna made. "It's coming," Anna whispered.

Sinty-ann nodded and quietly went about helping the baby to slide into the world.

In a little while she held up the baby for his mother to see. "He is a good boy," she said. She cleaned the baby and wrapped him snugly in the white cloths Anna pointed out to her. She tucked the baby in close to his exhausted mother. Then she went out to tell the others the news.

In the distance she could see Isaac coming with Mrs. Bigelow. She smiled to herself; Mrs. Bigelow would have little to do now. She looked around for Uncle, the baby's grandfather. He is the one who should be given the traditional announcement: "It is your close friend." That is how the news of a son was always given. A girl would have been announced more simply, "It is a girl," because boys were of course preferred. And then the women who had been singing the melancholy songs would change to a joyous tune. But there was no telling how these people did such things.

Instead of the grandfather, Lucy was the first one to receive the news. She had been hovering outside the cabin with Sarah and James and Prairie Flower. The little girls had their dolls, and James was—well, it was not clear what James was doing. Teasing them, probably. When her sons were the age of James, they had their own ponies; they were busy playing games that would teach them how to be warriors. They were not hanging around the house, watching girls play with their dolls, and teasing them.

Sinty-ann was glad, for Anna's sake, that the new baby was a boy. As much as she loved Prairie Flower, she believed it was always better to have a boy. Much more attention and affection were lavished on a son than on a daughter. And boys were indulged, allowed to do whatever they wanted.

Now there were six children in Anna's family. Sinty-ann envied her: Anna was fortunate to have so many. The women of the People had few children. Sinty-ann had been much admired in her tribe because she had given her husband three children. Most women were lucky to have two.

Lucy came shyly to the steps of the cabin and gazed up at Sinty-ann, waiting for news. "You have a brother," Sinty-ann told her.

Lucy smiled. "And is he healthy?" she asked. "Mama has lost two infants that were not."

Sinty-ann hesitated. The baby boy had not cried as lustily as she wished, but he seemed all right. "I think he is strong. You come and meet him."

Lucy followed her into the cabin. Martha, who had gone to weed the garden, threw down her hoe and hurried to join them. The younger children tiptoed in and gazed in silent awe at their sleeping mother and the tiny, red-faced bundle next to her.

But then Papa came with Mrs. Bigelow, who bustled in and shooed them all away, including Sinty-ann. Would this woman know to find sage to burn, to purify the room where the birth had taken place? Would she know to take Anna to the creek to bathe, to purify her body after the delivery? Sinty-ann supposed not. These white women seemed to know little about the importance of such things.

Oddly enough, no one asked her where she had gone. With the excitement of the birth, her disappearance seemed to have been forgotten. That night when all had settled down again, Sinty-ann listened to the breathing of the Parker family sleeping on all sides of her and remembered her own children, how they had come into the world, how joyously they had been received, first the two boys, and then many seasons later, her precious Topsannah. She had lost everything else, her husband, her sons, her People, her way of life. But at least she had her Prairie Flower.

She lay there thinking of what had happened to her in the wilderness for the past few days, of the panther that had become her *puha*, but mostly of the memories that had come back to her of her childhood. There was so much to occupy her mind, so many questions. Would her People have done the things that she remembered—to her own family? She knew the answer: she had been with them on raids, she had seen it with her own eyes, she had taken part in it. It was what the People did.

There had never been talk of "right" and "wrong" as there was in this family, where the parents read from a book they called the Bible and insisted that she and Prairie Flower must learn parts to recite: *Blessed are the poor in spirit: for theirs is the kingdom of heaven. Blessed are they that mourn: for they shall be comforted. Blessed are the meek: for they shall inherit the earth. Blessed are they which do hunger and thirst after righteousness: . . .* Then there was the other thing they always wanted her to say: *The Lord is my shepherd; I shall not want. . . . Our Father Who art in heaven, hallowed be Thy name.* She turned her mind away from that.

Her People didn't think about right and wrong. They simply lived their lives, hunting buffalo and making war on their enemies. The white settlers were their enemies. They had come onto the land where the People hunted their food. They had cleared away the trees, killed the game, built ugly cabins like this one, surrounded the land with fences so that neither the animals nor those who hunted them could roam freely.

She had heard the old men of the tribe talking: when the white men came, everything changed. They had to be driven out. She had been part of a white family, and the People had taken her away. It had been difficult for a while, but she had become part of them. She still did not understand why the white soldiers had captured her at the camp by the river or why Uncle had brought her here. Maybe that had been a misunderstanding. But why did they not let her go now when they knew she didn't belong here? Why would they not let her return to her People where she belonged?

Uncle had promised she could go, but now there was a war, "the war between the states," Uncle called it. Everyone talked about it, but Sinty-ann did not understand any of it. Something about the right to own slaves, Uncle explained. That much she understood: the People always had slaves. When someone captured someone else, the captives became slaves. She didn't know where Uncle had captured the dark-skinned people who were his slaves and worked in his fields.

She resolved never to speak of what she had remembered in the wilderness. Not even to Lucy. A young girl with much wisdom, she could nevertheless not be expected to understand Sinty-ann's torment, the conflict she felt. The memory was too painful, and she willed herself to forget what had happened long ago and could not be changed.

Ben had killed the panther, meaning to save Sinty-ann's

life, or Lucy's. He didn't know that the panther was Sinty-ann's *puha*, her medicine. For a short time she had had medicine, but she was sure it was gone now, gone forever. As the life of the panther left its body, surely the *puha* left hers.

She lay for a long time thinking about these things, and finally she slept.

In the days that followed the family was caught up in the new life that had come to them. They decided to name the baby Daniel. He was a quiet baby and seldom cried, but he was small and needed to be fed often. Sinty-ann had hidden a little bunch of crow feathers under the mattress to ward off the evil spirits that might be troubling him.

"Grandfather built this cradle," Lucy told her one afternoon as they sat on the long, shady gallery. Lucy rocked the cradle with her foot while she sewed. She was working on a cover for Martha's bed, stitching together small pieces of left-over cloth. Sinty-ann recognized scraps of her own calico dress. It was to be a gift when Martha married Jedediah. Sinty-ann was sewing new moccasins for Papa and Uncle.

"All of us have slept in this cradle," Lucy said. She broke off a thread and looked at Sinty-ann. "What did your babies sleep in? Did they have a special bed?"

"Cradleboard," Sinty-ann explained. She liked to tell Lucy about this, because it pleased her to recall the birth of her sons and the pleasant days when they were infants. "I make a bag of buckskin, very soft, and it is fastened to a board in the back. I wrap the baby in rabbit skin with dry moss to catch his mess, and I tie him in the cradleboard with leather thongs. All day he is in his cradleboard, and I carry him on my back or I prop him in a safe place when I do my work. At night I take him out and clean him and put him in his night cradle. It is made of stiff rawhide so that he can sleep in same bed with me, but I will not roll on him and harm him. He is happy. I am happy."

Lucy stared at her incredulously. "All the time in a cradleboard, tied up like that? When did you let him out?"

"When he is older I let him out to crawl around. Then he learns to walk. When he walks, his father puts him on a horse, and he learns to ride. By the time he is like James, he has his own pony. He plays games with other boys on their ponies. It is how he learns to be a great hunter. You see my boys, you understand."

"But James is only six! He is just now learning to ride!"

Sinty-ann allowed herself to smile at Lucy. "You see my boys," she repeated, "you understand."

"Tell me about them, Sinty-ann," Lucy said. "Tell me how Comanches learn." Everyone else was away from the cabin, except Anna, who was sleeping, or Lucy would not have dared to ask her such questions. Sinty-ann knew that Lucy had been told not to speak to her about her life with the People. "Comanches," these white people called them. Sinty-ann had tried to explain to Lucy that it was a name given them by their enemies, but sometimes Lucy forgot and used it anyway.

"First the boy learns to ride his pony," Sinty-ann said. "From then on, he is on his pony all the time. He doesn't use a saddle. He has to herd his father's ponies. He learns to use a rope to catch horses. His grandfather makes him a bow and blunt arrows and teaches him to shoot because father is out hunting and grandfather has more time to teach. He shoots birds and little animals. He grows bigger; he learns more. When he is like Ben, he moves to his own tipi. My son Quanah killed his first buffalo when he is your age. We had a celebration for that. Pecos was older, like Ben."

She continued, "First a boy becomes a good hunter, then he is a good warrior. He knows how to ride using his pony as a shield. He hangs over the side of the pony, one foot hooked over the pony's back, but he can still shoot an arrow. And he learns to rescue a fallen comrade, to pick up the body of a man, wounded or dead. Boys practice together. First they learn to ride in at full speed and pick up something from the ground, an old buffalo robe at first and then something heavier until they can pick up a grown man and put him on a horse. And if there is no one to help, he must be able to do this alone. It is a man's highest duty to his comrades."

Lucy had stopped sewing. "But why?" she asked, leaning intently toward Sinty-ann, forgetting about the quilt in her lap, forgetting to rock the cradle.

"A man of the People must not allow the body of another warrior to be scalped. This would allow the dead man's soul to escape. There would be no peace for him."

"Then why do they scalp other people?"

"Because they are enemies."

She stopped suddenly, thinking again of her husband and sons. As many hairs as grew on her head, that was how often she wondered where they were, if they were alive. After a moment Lucy sat back and resumed her sewing, her foot once again rhythmically rocking the cradle.

Sinty-ann glanced down at the tiny baby in the cradle and looked quickly away. He was not strong; he would not do well.

The crow feathers might help. Her People would give a sickly child a new name, hoping to change his fate.

She wondered if she should say this to Lucy, but in the end she said nothing, and the two of them sat in silence, each locked in her own thoughts.

CHAPTER SEVENTEEN

From Lucy's diary, August 31, 1861

*T*his morning we buried little Daniel John Parker, aged twenty days. We wrapped him in an embroidered cloth that Mama had been saving for a special occasion—but not this—and laid him in the tiny coffin Papa made for him. Papa dug a small grave beneath the hackberry tree in back of the cabin and placed the little wooden box in it. Then Grandfather read from his old Bible: "I will lift up mine eyes unto the hills, from whence cometh my help. My help cometh from the Lord, which made heaven and earth." When he finished the Psalm, he led us in prayer. We each took turns throwing dirt on the coffin. Mr. and Mrs. Bigelow had come with some chicken potpies. We ate and visited for a while, and then it was over.

We have known for some time, perhaps from the very beginning, that Daniel was a frail baby. His cries were weak, and he did not nurse strongly. But we all hoped that somehow he would survive, that we would care for him so tenderly and so well that he could not help but live. Mama and Papa and Grandfather have prayed for him constantly since his birth. But none of this appears to have done one bit of good, and yesterday he left this life as quietly as he came into it. I suppose it was meant to be.

Papa hides his feelings and goes out to work in the fields. Mama weeps, of course, but she also is exceedingly angry. At first she would not say why she was so riled, and we thought she was bitter because God had taken away her child. But finally she admitted to us that she blames Cynthia Ann for harming the infant, for putting some Indian spell on him. Although we have tried to tell her that this is nonsense, she refuses to listen to reason.

This is Mrs. Bigelow's doing. She found feathers, crow feathers, I believe, hidden in Daniel's cradle, and she leaped to the conclusion that it was a spell. That's what she told Mama. I know that Mrs. Bigelow has been frightened of Cynthia Ann ever since our trip to Austin in the spring. Of course she also remembers well that Cynthia Ann stole two of their horses on her first attempt to run away shortly after she came to us.

Mrs. Bigelow claims she still sees something wild and untamed in Cynthia Ann's eyes. She does not see what I see: that Cynthia Ann is not the same person she was back then. Mrs. Bigelow was insistent that teaching her Bible verses would subdue this wildness, but she is not yet satisfied that her plan is working. And because Mama needs to blame someone for her heartbreak, it is an easy thing for her to put the fault on poor Cynthia Ann.

I tried to explain this to Cynthia Ann and begged her to stay away from Mama. Actually I did not tell her the whole truth; I simply said that Mama is grieving deeply and that she wants to be left alone. And Cynthia Ann seems to understand. She admitted the business about the feathers to me—that she always tied a little bundle to the cradleboard when her children were babies. But Mama did not want to hear about it.

This is not all of the bad news. The war continues, and the situation worsens. Jedediah has heard from his friend Sul Ross that Texas has already raised ten regiments to serve the Confederacy. Mr. Ross has gone in, and Jedediah has told Martha that he plans to join as soon as he has helped Papa with the cotton. She is quite beside herself, but she is determined to put on a brave face. Now it seems that they will marry earlier than planned, but of course this is not the time to speak of a wedding, with so much sadness in the family.

I do not understand all the reasons for this war, although Grandfather and Papa and Jed do discuss it quite often. It has to do with states' rights, among them the right to keep slaves, which are sorely needed by cotton farmers like us and must surely not be taken away from us. Everyone here blames the President of the Union, Mr. Lincoln, for bringing us to this. Grandfather is a friend of Sam Houston, who was our governor until last spring, and like Mr. Houston was opposed to secession of Texas from the Union. But it has happened, and now the men are going off to fight. And I can see that Jedediah is impatient to go.

Grandfather says we must all be prepared to make sacri-
fices, that our lives will become harder, but we must not complain. Martha, of course, is sacrificing a life with Jedediah, and
I have promised Grandfather that I, as a loyal Texan and
daughter of the Confederacy, will do all I can to help.

CHAPTER EIGHTEEN

*S*inty-ann was the first one to spot the smoke, a thin wisp curling up from the direction of the Bigelows' cabin. The weather had turned cooler, and neighbors and friends from as far away as Fort Worth had gathered outside under the trees for the wedding of Martha and Jedediah. It was rare for so many to get together, as the settlers' farms are widely separated. Most planned to spend the night. They were all enjoying themselves; even Anna was smiling, although the spot under the tree behind the cabin was still a bare mound of earth, a stark reminder of the baby who had lived a short time and died.

Sinty-ann knew that she was blamed for the baby's death. It was, she was certain, Mrs. Bigelow's influence. Sinty-ann understood Anna's bitterness; the loss of her child had addled her thinking. But she did blame the Bigelow woman, who made up stories about her and poisoned Anna's fevered mind. Anna took in Mrs. Bigelow's poison and believed her. And so when Sinty-ann saw the curl of smoke in the distance, she said nothing. Maybe she was mistaken about the source.

Everyone had brought food, turning the event into a feast like the ones the People had after a buffalo hunt or a successful raid. The men had set up tables in the yard, laying boards across sawhorses and setting planks on rounds of logs for makeshift benches. The Bigelows had arrived first to help with the cooking, and Mr. and Mrs. Nathaniel Raymond and Mr. and Mrs. John Henry Brown and their families had all come shortly after. Soon quite a crowd had gathered.

Sinty-ann had helped the men dig the pit where they roasted a steer killed for the occasion. The women had baked chickens and wild turkeys, and they brought cakes yellow with butter and eggs and pies made with nuts, as well as all kinds of other dishes prepared with vegetables from their gardens. Everyone contributed to the meal.

When the work was done they all changed into their best clothes. Sinty-ann put on the silk dress they had made for her to wear to Austin, even though it was hot and heavy and uncomfortable. Prairie Flower was dressed up in a little dress that had been Sarah's with tiny yellow and green flowers, and Lucy had tied Prairie Flower's long, dark hair in two bunches with yellow ribbons.

Uncle had managed to buy enough cloth in Fort Worth for Martha to make a wedding dress. "You'd better take care of these clothes," he warned them, "because with the war on there's bound to be shortages." He had heard talk in the dry-goods store that the North was setting up a blockade, stopping the shipment to the South of cloth and other necessities produced in the North.

Poor Martha! For the past few days she had been sewing steadily, and her eyes were red both from sewing and from weeping because her new husband would soon be leaving her.

A man they called "preacher" had ridden out from Fort Worth to read from the Bible and to listen while Jedediah and Martha made promises to each other while every one stood by, listening. Sinty-ann noticed tears in the eyes of many others besides Martha.

But then, after one of Uncle's long prayers and another by the preacher, the feasting began and the mood lifted. Martha, hanging on Jedediah's arm, smiled sweetly and chatted with the guests, moving from group to group. But as soon as the bride moved on, the talk grew serious.

Sinty-ann idly listened, but it was always about the war, and she cared little about any of that. The war was the reason Uncle gave for not allowing her to return to the People. The war was the reason Jedediah was going off in two days to join one of the cavalry units, leaving his new wife behind.

The family had pitched in to help them finish their cabin, even the youngest children whose job was to mix the mud and sage grass to build the chimney. Prairie Flower had squealed with joy as she tramped around in the mess of water and clay to make the thick, sticky mixture. The older ones pushed her out of the way when it came time to form the lumps they called "cats and bats," packed around the wooden twigs that formed the chimney.

And Lucy had managed to get done piecing her quilt in time to have the neighbor women come to spend a day stitching it on a big frame lowered from above Anna's bed, so that it was ready to spread on Martha's new mattress ticking.

After the wedding they would spend two nights in their cabin, and then Jedediah would leave to join his regiment, and Martha would come back to stay with her family until he returned.

"It's only for a year, at most," Jedediah told the wedding guests. "We'll knock those Yankees into a cocked hat in much shorter time than that, you mark my words."

Then the subject changed to Indians, and Sinty-ann paid closer attention.

"I've heard tell the raids are starting up again," Mr. Raymond was saying.

"We can expect more trouble," Uncle said. "Ever since Fort Cooper closed last February and troops have been withdrawn from the other military forts, we're virtually without protection here."

"True enough," Jedediah said. "And it's my guess it'll get worse before it gets better."

So her People were raiding in the area again, Sinty-ann thought. She glanced again at the wisp of smoke that had thickened into a gray puff floating above the horizon and was certain now what it meant: her People must have raided the Bigelows' farm.

Her heart thumped. They were that close! She knew how close it was because she had taken horses from the Bigelows last winter. It might be her husband or her sons in the raiding party. Perhaps they would come for her. Perhaps they had somehow found out where she was, and they were on their way here!

But then she realized they would not have stopped at the Bigelows' farm first if they were coming here for her and Prairie Flower. Her spirits fell. Her People had no idea where she was. They would never find her. They would never know how close they had come.

The wedding celebration was nearly over and people who lived close by were getting ready to leave when someone else sighted the plume of smoke in the distance. Everyone knew immediately what she knew, and in no time the men had all saddled their horses and ridden away toward the Bigelows' farm, leaving the women to stare at the remains of the food.

Mrs. Bigelow turned on her in sudden fury. "You!" she shrieked. "Heathen! It is your savage friends who have done this!" And she collapsed in a heap. Martha rushed to her side, ignoring Sinty-ann, and Anna merely stared blankly, shaking her head as though she could not believe more trouble could befall them.

Lucy came and took Sinty-ann's hand and gazed at her sadly. "It is not your fault," she said gently, soothingly. "You are not to blame, Sinty-ann."

Sinty-ann studied the pretty, yellow-haired young girl who looked up at her with such tender concern in her clear blue eyes, and a familiar chord played softly across her memory.

"Lucy," she said finally. "My mother's name was Lucy. Like you."

CHAPTER NINETEEN

From Lucy's journal, October 15, 1861

Oh, what I would not give to write about a happy occasion in this unfortunate book! Although Grandfather reminds us every day that we have much to be thankful for, the truth is that our lives are quite dismal except in the smallest of ways, like a pretty sunset or a sweet smile from Sarah or Prairie Flower.

I'm sure Mr. and Mrs. Bigelow have little to be thankful for, except perhaps for the fact that they were here at the wedding and not at home when the Comanches swept in and set fire to their fields and cabin and destroyed everything they own. The Indians stole their horses, of course, but killed all the other animals. The Bigelows' two Negroes, old Ed and his wife, managed to hide until it was over and did survive. We saw the smoke during the wedding celebration, and the men immediately set out on their horses to investigate. They met the frightened Negroes on the road, almost too upset to give a complete description of what had happened.

So now the Bigelows must start over. Jedediah gallantly offered them his newly completed cabin until they can rebuild their own. Unfortunately the reason his cabin is available is that he left at dawn to join up with his regiment. Martha, utterly inconsolable, has come back to live in our sad household.

Mama still mourns the death of little Daniel. The truth to tell, she has not been herself since he died, and at times I fear she is not quite right in the head, convinced as she is that it was somehow all Cynthia Ann's fault.

Ben is in a bad temper because he wanted to go with Jedediah. Of course with but one arm he has been refused, even though he rides as well as anyone and shoots nearly as well.

And, hard as it is to believe, Cynthia Ann is grieving afresh because she is certain it was her people who are responsible for the ruin of the Bigelows' farm. But she does not grieve for the Bigelows (and I cannot truly blame her, because Mrs. Bigelow treats her horribly). She is mourning because her people passed so close by and did not know that she was here!

Before he left to join his regiment, Jedediah reported rumors circulating among the traders that Peta Nocona had died from an infected wound and that Pecos had been taken by a fever. It was also rumored that Quanah had gone to live with another band of Comanches, the Quahadas. Cynthia Ann showed little interest in this news, possibly because she did not trust Jedediah to report the truth, possibly because she chose to hide her true feelings—but news of Comanches nearby is a different matter. The intensity of her grief at this shows me that she is still much a part of them, and they are part of her, far more than she is of us or we of her.

And so, with all this misery around me, I do not know what to do or where to turn or to whom to speak. I cannot talk to Mama or to Martha, and Cynthia Ann is beyond my reach. Finally I went to Grandfather and told him how I felt. He is a kindly person, indeed, but what could he say but "This too shall pass, my dear Lucy. Pray, and this too shall pass." Although I wish deeply to believe that Grandfather is right, and I continue to be faithful in my prayers, somehow I feel that God is not now, and has never been, much concerned with the fate of the Parker family.

CHAPTER TWENTY

*S*inty-ann watched as Uncle showed off the apparatus. "It's a hand gin," he told the women—Anna and Lucy and Martha, and now even Sarah. "See, you crank it like this." He demonstrated, dropping a fistful of cotton bolls in the top of the wooden box and turning the handle. "Much better than picking out the seeds and hulls with your fingers, eh, Martha?" He shoved the contraption toward her.

"I suppose so," Martha answered in a listless tone that had become familiar to Sinty-ann. Ever since soon after the wedding when Jedediah left to fight the war, Martha had been gloomy. This was not the way a Nerm woman behaved when her husband left on a raid. Sinty-ann remembered well how proud she had felt when Peta Nocona had ridden off with the other warriors! The dangers were great. Men were often killed or badly wounded. But their women did not carry on like this!

Sinty-ann turned away. She would learn about the hand gin later, as she had learned about the walking wheel used for spinning cotton into thread and the loom for weaving thread into cloth. The loom and wheel had been stored in the shed, forgotten, until Uncle got them out and told the women they must learn to use them—"the way it was in the old days," he said. Because of the war, he explained, they would have to make their own cloth or do without. The loom and wheel had not been used in many seasons, not since Uncle's wife had died. None of them knew how to spin or weave, but they soon learned.

The war was the cause of much misery—Sinty-ann understood that. She saw that she was not the only one to suffer.

"Sinty-ann," Uncle said to her privately. "I haven't gone back on my promise to you. But it's impossible now. When peace comes, then we'll go. You understand?"

She nodded, observing the worry in his eyes. "Uncle," she said, as he was turning to leave, "when you kill a deer, please give the skin to me."

He said he would. Not long after their conversation, he brought two fine deer hides. She immediately set to work, removing the hair, smoking the skins to make the rain run off, stretching and rubbing them with soap (at last she had found a use for their soap) until the skins were as soft as cloth. Then she cut them up and stitched the pieces with sinew to make leggings and a shirt.

The women watched curiously as she worked, but only Lucy asked a few careful questions. "It's quite handsome, Sinty-ann. What are you going to do with it?"

Sinty-ann brushed the questions aside. It was her secret.

They looked astonished when she handed the finished buckskin suit to Ben without a word. Ben seemed completely confounded, but finally he managed to mutter, "Thank you," and left to try it on. She had sewn it so cleverly that the emptiness of the right sleeve was not apparent.

As soon as Lucy had a chance without the others around to hear, she whispered, "Why did you give that suit to Ben?"

"He is unhappy because he cannot go to fight," Sinty-ann explained. "I know how a man of the People feels when he cannot fight. And so I make him a present."

"But he killed the panther!"

She shrugged. "It doesn't matter. I remember the panther in my heart."

CHAPTER TWENTY-ONE

From Lucy's journal, December 30, 1861

I am doing my best to appear brave, for everyone's sake, and because my father wishes it so. Papa has joined Col. Clark's regiment and leaves tomorrow.

For the past two weeks, since Papa made his decision to fight for the Confederacy (although at forty years of age he would not have been conscripted), we have all been quite busy making his uniform—ginning, carding, spinning, dyeing, and weaving the cloth before we begin to cut and sew. Martha, Mama, Cynthia Ann, and I took turns, shifting from one task to another, working night and day with little rest. Even Sarah takes her turn now. A bleak and cheerless Christmas it was.

But at last we finished, and my father looks very handsome in his new outfit. Were it not for the sadness that accompanies his departure, I should be quite proud of him.

With Papa gone, there will be only Ben and Grandfather to keep the farm going, and we all do our best to make up for the privations we suffer. I did miss having sugar in my tea, but now we have no tea, so missing the sugar will no longer be important.

Martha feels that life is most unfair, for she has seen a husband off to war and now a father, and therefore judges her suffering to be twice as great as anyone else's. It is a momentous event when a letter arrives from Jedediah, which happens infrequently, and then she goes off by herself to read it and comes back drenched in a mixture of joy at having heard from him and misery that he is far away and in grave danger.

Mama, needless to say, is despondent. Papa's leaving is one more blow for her to bear. She will have nothing to do with Cynthia Ann or even Prairie Flower. I am sure it seems unjust to her that her own infant sickened and died while the little daughter of a woman she has come to fear and despise blooms with good health. Sometimes Cynthia Ann forgets and calls her little girl by her Indian name, although I think Prairie Flower is such a pretty name and suits her well. Every time she slips and says Topsannah, Mama rebukes her, if only with a sharp look. Prairie Flower is the only soul in this household who is unfailingly cheerful, perhaps because she is the only one too young to understand all that is happening. Were it not for her sunny disposition, I am sure we would all wither away.

Although Cynthia Ann has learned to spin and weave (along with the rest of us!), she much prefers to work with animal skins and has made a beautiful buckskin suit. I supposed she was making it to take to her son when at last this dreadful war is over and Grandfather allows her to go back for a visit to her people. We were all amazed when she gave the suit to Ben. Ben was more pleased than he let on and now seems more kindly disposed toward Cynthia Ann, but I fear that nothing will soften Mama's heart.

Cynthia Ann has promised to teach me how to prepare the skins, for I have in mind to learn to make buckskin gloves to sell. They wear well, and I believe it is a way for me to earn a penny or two for the family. God knows we will need every cent in the difficult days that lie before us.

Last evening as we rushed to finish Papa's extra shirts, an activity that served to keep us from our weeping for a time, Grandfather told us that he has written to Cynthia Ann's younger brother, Silas, Jr., who lives several days' journey to the east of here. (There is also a sister in east Texas, but I know little of her, and of course Cynthia Ann knows nothing of her at all.) Grandfather expects a visit from Silas as early as next month. Cynthia Ann made no response to Grandfather's announcement.

"Do you remember your brother Silas?" I asked her.

"He was just a little boy," she said after a time. "Running, playing, laughing. Like Topsannah. That's what I remember."

And so we wait for Silas's letter, too.

Now all of us will be waiting and praying for letters and must listen to Ben's angry muttering that because of a rattlesnake he is not able to go. But Mama is positively grateful to the snake since it means keeping her oldest son at home!

Cynthia Ann has been with us now for nearly one year. In some ways everything is changed, in others ways all is the same.

She is able to speak our language very satisfactorily but chooses to say little. She seems less wild than a year ago, but is she really? Grandfather believes yes, Mama most definitely no.

We can only pray and wonder what the coming year holds for us all.

Part III

CYNTHIA ANN

CHAPTER TWENTY-TWO

*S*ilas came in winter. Cynthia Ann was out on the gallery when the rough wooden cart drawn by a team of oxen clattered into the yard. She stared at the squarely built man and the boy perched on the seat next to him. Both carried rifles. The boy, with big ears and a shock of sun-bleached hair, swung down first. Silas followed slowly.

This is my brother, Cynthia Ann thought, mildly curious.

She believed he noticed her standing on the gallery, although he gave no sign. Instead he crossed the yard to the corral and greeted Uncle, shaking his hand. Something about the way he walked, a swing to his broad shoulders, the way he held his head at an angle, all this reminded her of someone. Her father, she decided. The boy, hands shoved deep in the pockets of his pants, looked nothing like him.

Silas turned, pushed his shapeless hat back on his head, and gazed up at her. "Cynthia?" he asked. "That you, sister?"

She stepped down the two wooden steps from the gallery and walked toward him. "I am Cynthia Ann," she said.

They looked at each other. Silas took off the hat and clutched the brim in his two hands.

"You well?" he asked finally. She nodded once, and he seemed satisfied.

Just then Prairie Flower skipped around from back of the cabin and beamed at the newcomers. "My child," Cynthia Ann said.

Now Silas turned his attention to the little girl who hugged her mother's legs. "Had one the same age," he said. "Lost her a while back." He pointed with the hat at the boy. "This here's my wife's nephew, Joseph."

Joseph regarded them with squinted, suspicious eyes. He turned to his uncle. "That your Injun sister?" he asked.

"This is your Aunt Cynthia. You be respectful, hear? She'll be coming home with us."

It was the first definite word she had had that she was to leave here and go there. The decision had been made without her, but it came as no surprise. She would be willing enough to go, to get away from Anna and all her raving about how Cynthia Ann was possessed and had caused the baby boy's death.

Cynthia Ann had not tried to persuade her otherwise. Among the People many babies died soon after birth. That was why women always hoped for a captive child to adopt when the warriors returned from a raiding party. That was why she herself had been adopted by Speckled Eagle and Calls

Louder. When a child died, the women grieved, howling and cutting their flesh with knives, and then they laid aside their grief for the dead child and went on with the business of living. But somehow Anna had not been able to do that. The grief had stayed buried inside her and gnawed at her until it burst out in anger and bitterness.

Later, Uncle came to talk to Cynthia Ann. "This is no good," he said, gesturing toward Anna, walking slowly to the henhouse wrapped in her ragged shawl, her chin sunk against her chest. "No good at all. Maybe you'll be happier with your brother. I'm sorry to see you go." He turned and left abruptly.

If she could not be where she belonged, then it was all the same to her if she stayed with Uncle or if she went to her brother Silas. But it made a big difference, it seemed, to Lucy, who burst into tears when she heard the news. "But I thought he was just coming to visit!" she cried. Although Cynthia Ann had begun to believe that she could never feel anything again, that all of the joys and sorrows had left her with the exception of her precious Prairie Flower, she *did* feel something when she saw how deeply Lucy was touched.

"Oh, let me go, too!" Lucy begged, tears streaming down her pale cheeks. "I know that I can be a big help to Uncle Silas and Aunt Mary, getting Cynthia Ann and Prairie Flower settled there, so they won't feel so lonely, and Aunt Mary won't feel as though she has complete strangers in her home."

It was plain that Anna did not want Lucy to go, that she feared letting one more member of her family out of her sight. It had already been decided that Ben must ride along with Silas for protection, after Silas's description of their narrow escapes on the way over, and that he must then join a westbound party to make the trip home safely. Since the beginning of the war and the withdrawal of the soldiers from the frontier forts, Indian raids had increased. Almost weekly they heard reports of new attacks at settlements along the unprotected frontier. Uncle said it was foolhardy for anyone to attempt the four-day trip without at least two armed men. But he did manage to convince Anna that Lucy might be safer once she reached east Texas than she was at home in Birdville.

At last Anna gave in, and Lucy brightened visibly. "Come, Cynthia Ann," Lucy said bravely, "we must mend your clothes and see about making some new ones." For the week or so that it took them to make their preparations, Martha helped. Anna seemed calmer. Silas and the boy helped Ben and Uncle to butcher a pig, mend fences, and put a new roof on the shed.

Then it was time for them to be on their way. They ate a last meal together, and once again Uncle prayed for all of them, for Isaac and Jedediah and the brave men of the Confederacy, and now for Silas and Joseph, and for Cynthia Ann and Tecks Ann, as he still called her, and for Ben and Lucy, who were setting out on a journey.

Prairie Flower, who had not yet gotten used to sitting quietly through these long prayers, squirmed and wriggled and began singing a little song Sarah had taught her. James did his best to make her laugh, teasing her until she began to giggle uncontrollably before the Amen. James managed to look completely innocent.

"Thank God you are leaving here!" Anna said loudly, interrupting the prayer. "I have little enough to be thankful for, but at least I can be grateful for that!"

Martha reached out sorrowfully and patted her mother's

arm, Lucy bit her lip and seemed to study her plate, and Sarah and James looked wide-eyed from one to the other. Silas appeared distinctly uncomfortable.

"There's been trouble, then?" he asked, turning to Uncle.

"Trouble? Nothing but trouble, where that one's concerned!" Anna said shrilly, her hard voice cracking.

"Oh, Mama," Lucy sighed. Her lip was trembling, and a pair of tears slid down her cheeks. Cynthia Ann looked away and gazed steadfastly past them all.

"It's been hard at times," Uncle said to Silas. "No one's to blame."

They ate in silence.

After the dishes had been washed and put away and the dishwater thrown out to the pigs, Cynthia Ann gathered her few possessions and waited to be told when they would leave.

"At first light," Silas said.

Cynthia Ann kept her eyes on the horizon. Prairie Flower curled up beside her, her battered rag doll clutched tight. Across from them, Lucy dozed against a heap of sacks. From the wagon seat, Silas guided the yoke of plodding oxen, cracking his whip and calling "Whoa-come!" and "Back!"

Next to him, Joseph kept turning around and peering over his shoulder at her until Silas said something that caused him to stare straight ahead again. He was supposed to be keeping watch as they made their slow, steady way eastward. Beside the cart, Ben rode his grandfather's horse, a rifle slung over his shoulder. Cynthia Ann knew he was watching out for Indians. So was she, but for a different reason.

The first night they stopped to camp near the settlement

of Dallas. Unable to find a farmhouse that welcomed travelers, Silas and Ben and the boy Joseph took turns staying awake as guards. Lucy crept close to Cynthia Ann to sleep, with Prairie Flower between them.

They ate simply, not bothering to build a fire, although Cynthia Ann had hoped they would. White people always built big fires, visible for miles. Perhaps some of her People would see and come for her. But now she realized that if some Nermernuh did attack this little company of travelers, they might mistake her for a white woman. They wouldn't know that she was one of the People unless she could call out to them first in their language. But what if she couldn't call out soon enough? For the first time, she understood the fear these white people had and even shared it.

On the second day, they joined the freight road that ran from Dallas to Shreveport. It was better than the road from Birdville, broader and not so rough—the stumps had been cleared away—and they made better time.

The second night they stayed at a farmhouse. After Silas introduced himself and the rest of his party and they had settled at the table with mugs of some dark liquid, a coffee substitute made from parched barley, the farmer and his wife hunched closer for a better look at Cynthia Ann.

"Too bad what those savages done to her," the grizzled old farmer said to Silas. "She looks like a strong worker, probably make a good wife, but there ain't a white man who'd want her after she's been with those Comanches. I remember when they brought your cousin Rachel Plummer back, that was probably twenty-five years ago. I knew her people, and they paid a ransom for her, but she was never quite right again." He tapped his forehead. "Died exactly a year after she come back, as I recall."

Rachel. Cynthia Ann remembered: a young woman with a baby, a little boy. Rachel and the baby were part of the memories she had pushed away. They were all captured together, carried off together, beaten and tormented. Then Rachel and the baby disappeared. So had the other woman, Mrs. Kellogg. And her own brother, John. He was Silas's brother, too. He had been sold to another band, as she recalled.

"Whatever became of your brother, John?" the farmer asked Silas. "There was a ransom out for him, too. But I don't think it was ever claimed."

"Turned Indian, best I know," Silas said. "Became one of them. Story we heard is he got sick, smallpox I believe it was, and the Comanche tribe that adopted him left him to die. But some little Mexican gal, one of their slaves, saved his life and nursed him back to health. He married her and went to live down south somewhere, near El Paso. They say he ranches there."

The old man shook his head. "You hear all kinds of things," he said.

His gray-haired wife was bustling around, preparing them a meal, but keeping a wary eye on Cynthia Ann. "Tell them what you heard, Ely," she instructed.

"Well," the farmer said, shifting his eyes toward Cynthia Ann, "a while back there was a trader stopped off here for a night. Told us Indian raids are picking up something awful out your way." He held out his tin cup to his wife to refill and watched as she poured the steaming brew. "Awful stuff," he commented. "Can't hardly stand to drink it. Anyways," he said, resuming his story, "this trader, Mr. Ennis, says there's a new young warrior leading these raids, raising all kinds of hell. Name of Quanah."

Cynthia Ann tried never to let the white people see how she felt about anything, but the news caught her by surprise. Her hand flew to her mouth, and she stood up suddenly, spilling her drink. The farmer's wife ran to get a rag to mop it up.

"Mr. Ennis says Quanah is this lady's son," he drawled. "Guess that answers my question."

On the fourth day they turned south, off the freight road, onto one much rougher with deep ruts and uncleared stumps. Heavy winter downpours turned the road into a muddy swamp. Swollen creeks had to be forded. Progress was slow.

They reached Silas's farm on the fifth day. As the wagon approached, Cynthia Ann saw a small, thin woman step out of the cabin, a baby in her arms and a little boy peeping out behind her skirt.

"That's Mary," Silas said. He had spoken very little on the trip. He lifted his hat, and she waved.

The wagon drew up in the yard, and the travelers stiffly clambered down. Mary stayed by the cabin door, motionless as a tree, until they all straggled up to her. Silas made introductions. "This here's Lucy, Cousin Isaac's girl—Isaac's gone off with the regiment—and Ben, his boy. And this here's my long-lost sister, Cynthia Ann, and her baby girl. Tecks Ann, some call her." He stepped back, and Mary peered at the newcomers.

Her gaze came to rest on Prairie Flower. "My, she sure does look Indian," Mary said flatly. "Is she filthy, like her people?" she asked Silas.

Silas coughed and looked down at his boots. "They've lived with Isaac's people for near a year now and learned their ways. They speak our language pretty good," he said.

But at that moment, Prairie Flower, who always chattered in English when she played with Sarah and James, suddenly turned to her mother and asked her something in the Nerm tongue.

Mary seemed shocked. She turned angrily to Lucy. "You mean your family let this child talk that savage language? I thought he said she'd been taught to talk proper."

Lucy glared at Silas's wife. "She can speak both," she said quietly. "Depends who she's talking to."

"Well, she can just forget that Indian talk altogether when she's living in *this* house," Mary said. "Come on in, then," she added brusquely and marched into the cabin.

Cynthia Ann clutched Prairie Flower's warm hand and slowly followed the sharp-faced little woman. Lucy trailed behind. Silas and Joseph had gone to unyoke the oxen, and Ben went with them to water his horse.

They had a plain supper of cornmeal mush and bacon, prepared by an old Negro woman, and ate without much conversation except for Mary's questions about how they were surviving the war in Tarrant County. Then it was time for bed.

"We planned on you and the little girl sleeping in that bed, Sister," Silas said.

"No need," Cynthia Ann said. "We sleep on this." She unrolled the buffalo robe and waited to be shown where to lay it. But Mary reacted as unhappily as Anna had when it first came to her cabin. Lucy intervened.

"It's what they always sleep on," Lucy explained. "It was her robe. She made it. It's very precious to her. It's quite clean, I assure you of that."

Mary regarded it doubtfully. Cynthia Ann watched her. If Mary refused to allow the buffalo robe, then Cynthia Ann would refuse to stay. She would insist on going back with Ben.

"Mary," Silas said quietly, pleading in his voice.

Mary threw up her hands in resignation. Cynthia Ann spread the robe in the corner farthest from the fire, and soon everyone had found a place to sleep. The only sound in the cabin was the deep, even breathing of the Parkers. Cynthia Ann lay awake, staring into the darkness. The old impulse was there again—*run*.

The impulse had never gone away. She had not stopped searching for a way to get back to her People. But she was watched too closely, and every attempt she had made had met with failure.

It was clear from the first meeting that she would get along no better with her brother's wife, Mary, than she had with Anna. Lucy would not stay here long. It made no sense to think of running, but that is what occupied her mind throughout the night. Perhaps Silas and Mary would not be so strict, she thought, or would not have the time to watch her so carefully. The distances were even greater now, she knew; she was far, far away from the land of the Nermernuh.

But now she knew for certain that Quanah was out there somewhere. Her son. She would not truly rest until someday, somehow, she would be with him again.

CHAPTER TWENTY-THREE

From Lucy's journal, January 21, 1862

When I persuaded Grandfather to let me travel here with Uncle Silas to stay with Cynthia Ann in her new home, I had not reckoned on what it would be like to be away from my family or to be here with this one. Ben stayed just long enough to eat and sleep and rest his horse, and then he joined a group of soldiers headed west to Fort Worth and left for home.

I longed to beg him to take me with him, but after going to so much effort to be allowed to make this trip, I could scarcely announce a change of heart.

I am not confident that things will go well here for Cynthia Ann and Prairie Flower, for it seems that this was Uncle Silas's idea and Aunt Mary makes only a grudging welcome to her sister-in-law and little niece and not much more to me!

It is a very comfortable home, a double log cabin like ours, but with four large rooms with high ceilings and a good stone fireplace. Grandfather's cabin, said to be the finest in Tarrant County, does not hold a candle to this. The furniture quite astonishes me; much of it was shipped all the way from New Orleans as a wedding gift. (Grandfather had given me to understand that Uncle Silas married a woman from a Louisiana family of considerable means.)

Mary brought many possessions from her family home in Shreveport, including a set of English bone china, which is displayed on a shelf built high up the wall. Her wardrobe of beautiful silk dresses is kept in a leather-covered trunk. She even brought her Negro, Silvy, who has taken care of her from the time she was in her cradle.

The farm is quite large, and with the help of several slaves, Uncle Silas has managed to clear a good portion of it to produce all kinds of crops. It would seem that Aunt Mary could want for nothing—although it's true, we all want for *something* with this dreadful war—but she complains constantly.

"If only we lived in Tyler!" she laments. Tyler is a large town a long day's ride to the east, where she describes well-stocked shops and a lively social life. "Before the war," she says, "we went there at least once a month to barbecues and cotillions. There was always something going on. Not like Shreveport, but better than *this*." She claims life is quite giddy in Tyler when the soldiers are home on leave and seems to regard the war as a serious inconvenience to her pleasure, since no one close to her here has had to go off to fight.

I was curious about that. Uncle Silas is several years younger than Cynthia Ann, much, much younger than my dear Papa and not so much older than Jedediah, both of whom are serving the Confederacy. Most of the men in this area, I have learned, have also gone off, leaving their wives in the most desperate straits as they try to manage farms and Negroes in the absence of the menfolk. However, Uncle Silas owns a tannery that has been requisitioned by the government to provide boots for our soldiers, and this keeps him safe at home. Yet his wife does not have the sense to be grateful for this good fortune but importunes him daily to take her to Tyler, to Athens, even to Ben Wheeler for an entertainment.

Silas is a sober, hardworking man whose patience is tested daily by his bad-tempered wife. (He and Cynthia Ann are the spitting image of one another. Silas is taller and thinner, but they have the same broad faces and stern mouths. It is their way of frowning deeply that particularly strikes me.) None of us escapes the lashings of Mary's sharp tongue—not Silas, nor Silvy, nor Cynthia Ann. Nor me.

Mary insists on calling Prairie Flower "Little Barbarian" and makes it plain that she does not want her young son Samuel or little Rose Ellen to associate with her. How she can resist those bright eyes and the dear smile is beyond me, but to Mary, Prairie Flower is simply another Indian, a savage to be despised. Like Mrs. Bigelow and Mrs. Raymond and our other neighbors in Birdville, Mary has begun a "scriptural cure," making Prairie Flower sit still for long periods each evening while she reads Bible verses to her and tries to make her memorize them.

Twice now since our arrival she has caught Prairie Flower speaking to Cynthia Ann in the Comanche language, calling her mother by her old Indian name, Naduah. Mary became furious, lost her temper, and slapped the little girl. But Silas says nothing or is not here when there is an incident, and it is not my place to interfere.

Cynthia Ann reacted quite calmly, seeming more sad than angry. "Don't hit her," she said both times and led Prairie Flower away. "She can speak however she likes." It is as though she has become resigned to her fate. But I don't know that she truly has.

She does her best to help out, understanding that these are difficult times. Soon after our arrival, Cynthia Ann told Silas, "I can gin and card cotton, spin, weave, sew—all these things. And I can prepare skins, make moccasins, harnesses, whips, everything. I will work hard."

He seemed to think about this, for his tannery makes nothing but boots nowadays, and ordinary citizens cannot buy shoes and must make do with what they have. (Mary frets that she will not have pretty slippers to wear to the fancy dress balls of Tyler if and when she does have a chance to go!) "All right," he said at length. "You can make moccasins for all of us, including the slaves. And help out Mary, if you will, please— do whatever other such work needs doing."

The next day Silas gave her a corner of his shed where he has assembled a few tools for leatherworking. In no time at all word spread to the nearby farms that she is here; everyone knows her story, it seems. The curious come to gawk at her and the child, and the visitors bring their broken harnesses to be mended or place an order for a whip or some other item of leather.

One gentleman drove all the way down from Grand Saline

with a couple of deerskins. She set to work immediately and soon had made a buckskin suit, which Aunt Mary bartered to the man for flour and other staples. Cynthia Ann gave me the scraps, from which I have fashioned a pair of work gloves for Uncle Silas, who seemed pleased. I can think of nothing to do for Aunt Mary that would be equally pleasing.

Now I have discovered Cynthia Ann's secret: while she does her leatherwork in the corner of the shed, she is teaching Prairie Flower her Indian ways. I was passing by on the path to the privy, heard quiet voices, and paused to listen. It was Cynthia Ann speaking to Prairie Flower in what I thought must be the Comanche tongue. When Prairie Flower answered in English, her mother corrected her. This interested me, for I have not heard her speak to her little daughter in that language since she made her promise to Grandfather in exchange for *his* promise to take her to her people. All of that is impossible now with the war, and since we came here we have put many more miles between Cynthia Ann and her people.

Over a year has passed since her rescue and return to her family, and I believe that running away is no longer uppermost in her mind. But if she has accepted her life and circumstances *for herself*, I believe strongly that she is preparing Prairie Flower as best she can so that the child can join her people when the time comes, whenever that may be.

And another secret: I have noticed that she and Prairie Flower go for walks in the piney woods nearby when the weather is mild and the work is done. The Negroes are to be guarding her by turns, but they are quite lackadaisical about it, believing, I suppose, that she would not go far for the same reason they do not: someone would surely find her and bring her back.

Yesterday I followed them. Cynthia Ann seemed to know exactly where she was going; it was not an idle stroll. I stepped carefully, keeping a good distance behind her. Presently they came to a little clearing. When they stopped, I crouched among the low growth. From this blind, I watched.

Using a tree branch as a broom, she swept off a place that seemed already smoothed. Then she marked a circle on the ground with a stick and drew other figures inside the circle that I could not make out. Meanwhile, Prairie Flower was sent to gather twigs and moss. I held my breath when she came in my direction, but she moved on without seeing me.

With a flint Cynthia Ann started a fire, so small that the smoke was unlikely to be noticed. From inside her shirt she drew something—a man's pipe!—and filled it with what I took to be tobacco, or perhaps a kind of herb, which she lit with a piece of kindling from the fire. *Where had she gotten the pipe? The tobacco? What was she doing?*

Having neglected to bring my warm shawl, I shivered with cold in my hiding place, my teeth chattering, but was too fascinated to leave. Cynthia Ann went on with her ritual, puffing on the pipe and blowing smoke this way and that. Then the two began singing softly, a sorrowful tune that tugged at my heart.

When it seemed they had finished, I slipped away quickly, returning to the cabin by a roundabout way. I had much to ponder. All of us believed that Cynthia Ann had truly found her way back to our ways and was bringing up the little Indian

Prairie Flower to behave like a white child, but she is, in fact, doing the opposite. How long has this been going on? I ask myself if I should tell Uncle Silas about the scene I have witnessed. And what good would it do? Perhaps he will discover it for himself. And I can only imagine the ruckus it will cause when Aunt Mary finds out!

CHAPTER TWENTY-FOUR

$\mathcal{A}$ll through the warm, damp days of spring, Cynthia Ann listened to them argue. Her brother Silas, a kindly, gentle man, was married to an angry, complaining wife who took him to task for everything that was not as she wished it, and that was a great deal.

"Why, oh, why," Mary would begin in a voice as sharp as a needle, "has it become my lot in life to live with this strange woman you claim is your long-lost sister and that little barbarian of hers?"

"Now, Mary," Silas would reply soothingly. "Please don't take on so. It's bound to get better, I promise you. It just takes some getting used to, some patience on both sides."

"Patience!" Mary would snort. "The good Lord has apparently left me well short of that!"

Cynthia Ann pretended not to hear their arguments. Mary sometimes yelled loudly and once hurled one of her delicate china cups—the ones she kept on the high shelf and used only for guests, the ones she would not allow Cynthia Ann to touch—against the cabin wall. When she saw the shattered blue-and-white fragments on the floor, Mary threw herself onto the bed and sobbed as though her heart were breaking. All over a china cup.

At these times Prairie Flower would stop whatever she was doing and run to hide in the privy. On the day that the china cup was smashed, the little girl fled to her hiding place and refused to come out, turning the wooden block nailed inside the door so it could not be opened from the outside.

"No!" she shouted when Cynthia Ann tried to coax her out.

"She will come out when she wants to," Cynthia Ann told the others, secretly pleased at her daughter's stubborn determination. But hours passed, and Prairie Flower stayed locked in the privy. Cynthia Ann went to talk to her again.

First she spoke in the white man's language. "Come out now," she said. "Not nice to stay in there."

"No," Prairie Flower said. "Stay here."

Then Cynthia Ann switched to the Nerm language, explaining that no one was going to hurt her. "Aunt Mary hit," Prairie Flower said. Cynthia Ann promised that she would not allow anyone to hit her, although she was not sure she could prevent it if Mary flew into one of her rages.

Prairie Flower began to cry.

"Open the door," Cynthia Ann begged. But she had only

Prairie Flower's sobs as a response. Finally she turned to Silas. "We must do it," she said.

Without a word Silas brought an iron bar and pried open the door, which then had to be taken down and repaired and put back up again. Prairie Flower crept out cautiously, looked around, and ran headlong into her mother's arms. Cynthia Ann soothed her, stroking her hair, whispering to her, and carried her to the corner of the shed where she felt secure.

That night Cynthia Ann heard them arguing again.

"I can't send them away," Silas said to his furious wife, whose belly was beginning to show another child. "They're kin. And besides, Mary," he added, "the legislature has made me her guardian. The hundred dollars a year comes to us now instead of to Uncle Isaac."

"I don't give *that* for the money," Mary stormed, snapping her fingers. "And as for being kin, I say they're not! After what she's done with those filthy Indians, she's not even white anymore—I don't care what you say! And look at that child! If ever there was a savage, it's that girl! People like them give up their right to be called kin, Silas. I can't believe you'd allow such people around your own children, and around me in my condition!" Then the rage gave way to tears.

For several days after that outburst no one spoke, and the cabin was filled with a heavy silence, the way the prairies sometimes got before a tornado whirled across the land ripping up a path of destruction.

Then it was as before. Mary made sure they got the leavings of their meals, serving them lesser portions on the same tin plates the Negroes used. When Silas was away at the tannery supervising the boot making for the army, Mary fed them in the lean-to with the Negroes.

Through all of this, as though she heard nothing, saw nothing, understood nothing, Cynthia Ann kept her face a perfect mask and did her work. She didn't know what would happen to her, and she didn't care. Everything now was for Prairie Flower.

All the white women from the beginning had insisted that Prairie Flower must speak only the white people's language. First it was Anna and Mrs. Raymond and Mrs. Bigelow and Mrs. Brown who made her recite those words from their book. And now Mary, who dared to slap her for using the Nerm language, for calling her mother Naduah.

Cynthia Ann had promised Uncle that she would learn the white people's language and ways in return for his pledge to take her back to her People. But she had promised him nothing about Prairie Flower. *Topsannah*. The child seemed to be forgetting her own name! The war had come, war among white men, a much bigger war than anything the People had ever known, and that kept her from going back. She didn't blame Uncle; she saw that he was truly sorry.

But now she knew that she must get Topsannah ready to return—tomorrow or in another winter or whenever the time came. The child must not forget her language, and already there were signs that she spoke the white man's language even more readily than her own. She must learn to prepare skins so that when she returned to the People she would be able to make clothing for her husband and children and tipi covers for her family, and she must learn to recognize wild plants to feed them when there was no meat.

When Prairie Flower came with her to the shed, she talked softly to her in their language, taking care not to let the others hear. Silas's boy Samuel was always looking for her to come and play, and she knew that Prairie Flower wanted to be off with him, but Cynthia Ann insisted. Every day she would teach her a little, so that she would not forget.

Lucy often came to the shed to work on some gloves. Sometimes Lucy appeared suddenly, and Cynthia Ann recognized by the look on her face that she had overheard them murmuring together. But she knew that Lucy would say nothing, certainly not to Mary, whom she disliked—that much was plain!—and probably not to Silas. Cynthia Ann had come to trust Lucy, young as she was, more than any of the white women she had met. And she was sad to think that Lucy would be leaving soon, returning to her own home, her own mother.

"I can't stay here long," Lucy told her while she stitched, "I came so that you would not be so lonely at first." She looked around. "But I'm afraid . . . ," she trailed off.

"Not lonely," Cynthia Ann tried to reassure her. "I have my little girl."

"I know," Lucy said. Then she took a deep breath, perhaps summoning her courage. "Your son Quanah is distinguishing himself among his people," she said. "You must have been proud to hear the farmer say that."

Cynthia Ann nodded but kept her eyes on her work. "His name means Sweet Fragrance," she said. "Quanah was my name for him. A good name."

"A good name," Lucy agreed, but her voice showed that something troubled her. "But why must he raid our settlements?" she burst out.

"It is what he does," Cynthia Ann explained, but she knew this didn't satisfy Lucy and that nothing would. "He is Nerm."

When a man from somewhere to the north brought deer-skins for a buckskin suit, Cynthia Ann managed to speak privately with him before he left.

"Do you have any tobacco?" she asked.

He looked at her oddly, a smile twitching the corner of his lips. "Picked up some bad habits from those Injuns, did you?" he asked.

"Do you have any tobacco?" she repeated as though she had not heard him.

"I'll bring some when I pick up the suit," he said. When he came back to collect his suit, he slipped the little packet of tobacco to Cynthia Ann with a broad wink.

Cynthia Ann hurried to the shed where she had hidden a pipe, one of Silas's, which she hoped he wouldn't miss. One or another of Silas's Negroes was supposed to be watching her, but she had explained to cottony-haired Jim, "No need for you to come. We're going for a walk. We will come back before sunset." The old dark-skinned man seemed relieved and nodded, turning away. Neither of them was free to leave, and both knew it.

Cynthia Ann and Prairie Flower ducked into the pine woods, which had a greenish light even in winter. Presently they came to the clearing they had prepared on earlier visits. Cynthia Ann swept off the circle, and sent Prairie Flower to gather kindling.

"Lucy," Prairie Flower whispered in the language of the

People, laying down a handful of dried grass. "In the bushes, watching."

Cynthia Ann didn't turn around. "That's all right," she said. "But we must not let her know we know she's there."

She built a small fire. From inside her shirt she drew out the pipe, tamped in a pinch of tobacco, and lit it.

"First," she told Prairie Flower, "we honor Father Sun by blowing a puff of smoke to him." She did this. "Then Mother Earth," she said, puffing again. Then she blew smoke to the east, west, north, and south, naming them as she did. Prairie Flower imitated her with a wooden stick.

When they had finished by singing a lament for her People, Cynthia Ann dumped dirt on the fire and carefully spread pine needles over the circle. "No hurry," she said to Prairie Flower. "We must give Lucy time to leave."

"Not tell Aunt Mary!" Prairie Flower chirped. "Not tell Uncle Silas! Not tell nobody!"

Hand in hand they returned to the cabin. They found Lucy calmly stitching on a knapsack for one of the neighbors who was leaving to fight. When Lucy raised her eyes, Cynthia Ann read the questions in them, but she turned away.

CHAPTER TWENTY-FIVE

From Lucy's journal, March 19, 1862

Grandfather and Ben arrived two days ago. We leave tomorrow—they are in a rush to get back to Birdville as soon as possible. I was in the shed with Cynthia Ann and Prairie Flower when we heard the clatter in the yard and the dogs yapping and people talking. I paid no attention, assuming it was someone to see Uncle Silas on business or a neighbor to order moccasins. We both kept on with our work, but Prairie Flower scurried off to investigate. Soon she returned, leading my weary-looking grandfather by the hand.

"Here's Naduah," Prairie Flower said, beaming, pointing to her mother.

My heart sank, knowing how he felt about the use of

Cynthia Ann's Indian name. Grandfather frowned. "Naduah?" he asked. "Is that what she calls you?"

Cynthia Ann jumped to her feet, aware, I'm certain, of his opposition. "Sometimes she calls me that," she admitted. "Are you well, Uncle?"

"Yes, yes, I'm fine, fine. But I've come for Lucy." He turned to me. "Your mother has taken a turn for the worse, my dear," he said gently. "You are needed at home. I wrote a letter, but the mail is undependable. Your work here is finished now, is it not? Cynthia Ann and Tecks Ann are comfortably settled here, then?"

Before I could reply, Cynthia Ann interrupted. "I must return to my People," she said bluntly. "They try to be kind, but I do not belong here."

Uncle shook his head sadly. "Out of the question, I'm afraid. We're in for a long haul. It may be a long time, Cynthia Ann. We have to make the best of it."

She tried to keep from showing her deep disappointment, but, of course, I knew. My own feelings were unsettled. I have been here more than two months and am more than ready to go home, but I shall miss my cousin and certainly her precious Prairie Flower. I am not sure that Cynthia Ann cares that I am leaving, at any rate not as much as I do.

I do hate to see her here! Even with Grandfather present, Aunt Mary makes scant effort to treat Cynthia Ann with more than bare civility, saying once to Grandfather, "They are nothing but savages, you know. Hopeless savages."

And Uncle Silas says only, "Mary's a mite touchy just now. Her condition," referring to the baby on the way.

There is a ray of hope. I know that Uncle Silas and Cynthia Ann have a sister who lives here in Van Zandt County, and it puzzled me that the sister, whose name is Orlena, has never been among the many visitors here. But little Samuel, in the way of children, let the cat out of the bag. "My mum and her had a fight," he told me. "A big one! I thought Mama was going to scratch her eyes out!" he went on, his own eyes wide at the memory. It is my hope that Orlena will be more of Silas's disposition than of Mary's, and that somehow Cynthia Ann and Prairie Flower will end up with them.

This afternoon after I had packed up my things, I went back to the shed to make my farewell to Cynthia Ann. "I want you to know that I shall miss you, and Prairie Flower, too," I told her. "I know how disappointed you are that you have not been able to visit your family because of this dreadful war, even though Grandfather promised that you could. But I want to make you a promise."

Only then did she look up at me. "I am young and only a girl at that," I rushed on, "but if I can find a way to bring you to your son, I promise you that I shall do it. I promise that I shall never stop looking for a way." I crossed my heart as I spoke.

For a moment, she said nothing but looked at me with those troubled eyes. Then she reached down and with a ragged fingernail scratched something in the dirt: PROMISS. One word that she remembered from the times I had tried to teach her her letters. She had seemed to take to reading and writing, but in recent months there was always so much work to be done and never enough time for our lessons. Yet she remembered this word.

I picked up a stone and scratched under it my name. She nodded, and then, before anyone could see it, I rubbed it out with my foot.

I have given my pledge without the least idea of how I will keep it. I will go with Ben and Grandfather with a heavy heart, knowing that the one blessing in Cynthia Ann's life is her precious Prairie Flower.

CHAPTER TWENTY-SIX

*T*he woman greeted Cynthia Ann with a bright, nervous smile, walked right up, and put her strong arms around her. "Hello, Sister," she said in a cheerful voice. "And this must be our little Tecks Ann."

"Topsannah," Cynthia Ann corrected her. "Prairie Flower in your language," she added.

"What a pretty name, Prairie Flower!" She knelt down and held out her arms. Prairie Flower walked into them and accepted the embrace. "Oh, she is just too precious!" Orlena cooed. "How can you bear to let them go, Mary?"

Mary struggled, Cynthia Ann saw, not to give it all away and end up having to keep them after all if she told the truth. "They don't like it here," Mary said flatly. "And with the new baby coming, it's too much."

"Well, I'm sure they'll be happy with us, won't they, Ruff?" She turned to the man with her, a tall, broad-chested man with wild red hair and a bushy beard.

The man swept off his broad-brimmed hat and bowed to Cynthia Ann. "Ruff O'Quinn, Miss Parker," he said. "And I am pleased to make your acquaintance. As my wife has said, we will do our best to make a good home for you and your daughter."

He replaced his hat and stepped back. Cynthia Ann looked him over carefully. Without a word she went to gather up her buffalo robe. She was ready to go, had been, in fact, since the hot, rainy night when Silas finally gave in to Mary's scolding.

"I simply can't bear it, Silas," Mary had cried. "That child might as well be a purebred Indian. She *looks* Indian, she *talks* Indian, she *acts* Indian, and her mother actually encourages her! Please, *please* send them away!"

"All right, Mary," Silas had said wearily. "I'll talk to Orlena and Ruff and see what they have to say." Orlena, Cynthia Ann remembered, was a sister, the baby in Mama's arms.

"Won't you stay and visit for a spell?" Silas asked now. "I believe Mary's fixed a nice dinner for us."

Cynthia Ann knew this was not true. They had been arguing about that, too, Silas insisting that his sister and brother-in-law should be offered a good meal and perhaps invited to stay the night. But Mary was in no mood for any of this. She simply wanted Cynthia Ann to leave, and the sooner the better. Maybe Anna had sent word that Cynthia Ann had cast a spell on the baby Daniel that made him sicken and die. She wanted Cynthia Ann out of any possible reach of her baby, due soon from the look of it.

But it was also clear that Orlena was not especially fond of her sister-in-law, either. Silas must have known they'd refuse, and Orlena's ruddy-faced husband had no objection to turning around and starting the journey back to a place they called Slater's Creek. She never even took off her bonnet, accepted only a tin mug of substitute coffee—Mary did not get down the fine china cups for them—and they were on their way.

Ruff O'Quinn's wagon was more comfortable than Silas's, and the well-fed mules stepped along smartly. Orlena kept turning around to make sure Cynthia Ann and Prairie Flower were all right, confiding over the rattle of the wagon wheels, "I hope you don't mind, Cynthia Ann, that we didn't stay. But I just could not wait to get away from there. My sister-in-law is a good Christian woman, I'm sure, but she and I don't see eye-to-eye on a good many things and, frankly, I spend as little time as possible around her."

Cynthia Ann nodded. "All right," she said.

"Now my brother, Silas"—she paused, laughed nervously, and began again. "That is, *our* brother Silas is a good man, exceptionally patient. But it just seemed you might be happier with us. Mr. O'Quinn was a widower when I married him, but his children are all grown and gone now, and the Good Lord has not seen fit to give me any children of my own." Here a shadow of sadness passed across her face, but she made a determined effort to be cheerful again. "It must be God's will that you and Tecks Ann are coming to live with us."

Cynthia Ann nodded. She could think of nothing to say to this.

———

It turned out that they did not plan to travel to Slater's Creek that evening but stopped instead in a settlement called Ben Wheeler to visit with friends. T. J. Cates and his wife, Amelia, were expecting them and had prepared a hearty meal. Mr. and Mrs. Cates were immediately charmed by Prairie Flower.

"Oh, what a lovely child!" Mrs. Cates cooed, scooping her up and carrying her around, although Prairie Flower was tired and grumpy from the trip. "She is simply the most precious little thing I've ever seen."

"Down," Prairie Flower said and lunged away from the strange woman toward her mother's lap.

"How old is this darling baby?" Mrs. Cates asked.

Orlena looked at Cynthia Ann for an answer. It was the kind of meaningless question white people liked to ask. Cynthia Ann remembered the night the baby was born, a hot night like this one. "We don't count," she said.

"About three, wouldn't you say?" Orlena suggested.

"Does she talk?" Mr. Cates asked, for the usually chattery Prairie Flower had said almost nothing.

"She talks."

"Maybe a good night's sleep will do the trick," Amelia Cates said cheerily and began to prepare beds for her guests.

If Mr. and Mrs. Cates and Orlena and Ruff O'Quinn were taken aback by Cynthia Ann's insistence on sleeping on her buffalo robe on the floor, they said nothing. But Cynthia Ann did overhear Mrs. Cates say quietly to Orlena before they resumed their journey the next day, "My dear, you do have your work cut out for you, I'm afraid. Forgive me for saying so, but your sister's mind has probably been addled by all she's gone through. I shouldn't wonder! But that child—I'd take her myself in a minute!"

"I think you can expect to see a lot more of us, Ruff," Mr. Cates boomed. "Seems as though Amelia here has fallen in love!"

Cynthia Ann took Prairie Flower up on her lap and held her tightly, her chin on her daughter's shiny hair. She didn't like what she had heard. What if these people who made a big fuss over Prairie Flower wanted to take her from her mother to raise as their own, the way Cynthia Ann had been taken away from *her* mother?

She remembered again her terror as a child—older than Prairie Flower, but still very young—when the men with the painted faces had seized her and dragged her away from her family. She must not allow this to happen to her child. She must be vigilant.

The first days in her new home were difficult even though Orlena was kind, completely different from Mary. She tried hard to make Cynthia Ann feel at home. There was work to do, of course; no one could afford to be idle.

"I can make moccasins," she told her relatives. "Fix harnesses. Make whips and reins."

But Ruff O'Quinn was not like Silas. His business, he explained, was lumber. He owned several sawmills. He offered to take her to visit one of them if she liked. Otherwise, she might help Orlena with the spinning and weaving. Ruff owned several slaves who worked in the mills, and all of them needed clothes. "Before this dreadful war, it was different," Orlena said. "But now we must make do however we can."

The first thing Cynthia Ann needed to find was a place away from the others where she could instruct Prairie Flower in the language and ways of the People. But those few stolen hours were not enough. Cynthia Ann watched in dismay as her daughter continued to learn to speak the language of white people, more every day. No matter how hard Cynthia Ann tried, it seemed that the white people's ways were taking over. She would not even be able to show her daughter how to make a tipi cover or how to prepare pemmican when she was older!

Every Sunday, the day that Ruff and Orlena gathered with a few of their neighbors to sing and read from their Bible, Mr. and Mrs. Cates came to visit, always bringing a gift for Prairie Flower—a little wooden dog, a new hair ribbon. Cynthia Ann made sure that she was present during these visits. Then one Sunday, Amelia Cates asked if they might take Prairie Flower visiting with them to other families in Ben Wheeler. "It will be good for her to be with children," Amelia said.

Cynthia Ann began to refuse. Then she saw Prairie Flower's mouth turn down at the corners. At last she agreed and paced restlessly until her child was returned to her at the end of the day.

The next week it was the same, and nearly every week after that. Prairie Flower loved it, but Cynthia Ann never felt easy until the visit was over and the Cateses had gone home.

"My land, you do get worked up about this, sister," Orlena chided her mildly. "Let her go! Let her enjoy whatever small pleasures she can!"

Cynthia Ann was silent. What could she possibly say to these white women that they could begin to understand?

Lucy would understand, but Lucy was far away, almost as impossibly far away as the People. Sadly Cynthia Ann acknowledged to herself that she might never see any of them again. But at least she had Prairie Flower, and someday Prairie Flower would return to the People.

CHAPTER TWENTY-SEVEN

From Lucy's journal, April 9, 1863

A year has gone by since I came back from Uncle Silas's, and a difficult year it has been for us all. Weeks pass in which we hear from no one and struggle along here in isolation, but yesterday Grandfather returned from Fort Worth bringing three letters. What an occasion! One was from Papa, from which we learned that he is now serving in Virginia. He claims that he is well and sends love to all of us. It was good to have the sight of his handwriting, but how much better it would be to have sight of *him*.

A second letter was from Jedediah, which Martha carried off to read alone. This is the first she has heard from him in nearly two months, and she has been quite beside herself with worry. He was sorely wounded, he writes, and his left leg had to be amputated at the knee. He has been lying in a hospital somewhere in Tennessee, out of his head with fever, but he is mending now and expects to be sent home to us soon. Martha cried and cried when she read about his wound, but now she is grateful to learn that he is alive and will be returning. Ben says that they will make a good pair, he with one arm, Jed with one leg.

The third letter came from Orlena O'Quinn, Cynthia Ann's sister in Van Zandt County. She writes that Cynthia Ann decided to leave Silas's place because of problems with his wife, Mary, and has been living with her and her husband, Ruff O'Quinn, at Slater's Creek since last September. Actually she had little to say about Cynthia Ann. Most of the letter is about Prairie Flower, who has captivated everyone. She says that a couple named Cates drives over from Ben Wheeler every Sunday afternoon to take Prairie Flower visiting with them around the countryside.

Orlena says they are rather well-to-do—Mr. Cates owns a salt mine—and they have provided the little girl with lovely clothes. This in itself is amazing considering that most of us here are ragged and making do with patches, and now patches on top of patches, a result of that Northern blockade. Grandfather believes that both Mr. O'Quinn and Mr. Cates are wealthy enough to have paid men to take their places in the army and are content to stay at home and let others fight in their stead. (Grandfather says it costs dearly to do so.) Much as we miss him, I am more proud than ever of Papa.

Prairie Flower "speaks beautifully," Orlena writes, which means, I suppose, that she has learned English well. I am certain that Cynthia Ann is unhappy about this because I know she was trying to teach the little girl her Indian tongue so that she would never forget her Comanche people.

Poor Cynthia Ann! I do still miss her, although I suppose it is for the best that she is safe with her sister, rather than sharing our dangers. There have been so many Indian raids that we have been advised to fort up, to band together and erect a stockade to protect ourselves. The Bigelows, who have been living in Jed and Martha's cabin, have been afraid to try to rebuild their burned-out home. Now that Jed is coming back, I imagine they will soon make other arrangements.

Every time there is a report of another raid, of more homes and fields destroyed, more horses stolen, I wonder: Is it Quanah? Is he the leader of these savage bands?

I worry about this because my brother Ben has sworn a solemn oath that although he was not fit to be a soldier, he can still be an Indian fighter, and he will not rest until he has rid the frontier of the Comanche leader. I fear that the leader he intends to kill is Cynthia Ann's son.

CHAPTER TWENTY-EIGHT

I don't know what ails her," Mrs. Cates said worriedly, untying Prairie Flower's bonnet. "She was fine while we were at my sister's, but just now when we were on our way to the Nelsons' she complained of a headache and said her stomach hurt. I thought she was just tired, but now I'm not sure."

Prairie Flower gazed up at her mother with eyes bright with fever. "I take her," Cynthia Ann said and picked her up. The little girl, normally so quick and energetic, sagged into her mother's arms.

"I sick," she whispered and laid her face close to her mother's neck. Cynthia Ann could feel the heat of her skin. She carried her to the buffalo robe in the corner of the cabin. Soon the child was asleep, but it was not her usual calm, peaceful sleep. She tossed restlessly.

Cynthia Ann stayed awake all night, bathing Prairie Flower's feverish face with cool water and trying to get her to take sips of a tea that Orlena brewed. She would waken for brief periods and then drift off to sleep again.

The days passed in a blur for Cynthia Ann. She never left her child's side, dozing fitfully herself on the buffalo robe, always alert when Prairie Flower made the slightest movement.

The days turned into weeks, which slipped by one after the other. Cynthia Ann knew that a week had passed when Mr. and Mrs. Cates came and sat with her beside Prairie Flower's bed. Twice they brought a doctor who examined the sick child and shook his head. "I'm sorry, ma'am," he said, "but there's nothing I can do."

Several times, a preacher stopped by, and the family knelt in a circle around the little girl, praying for an end to her illness. Cynthia Ann merely stared past them at her daughter.

The nights lengthened. Winter came. The child grew weaker, racked with fever and chills, tormented by a cough that gave her no rest. Her breathing became more ragged.

If she dies, Cynthia Ann told herself, *then I die too; I have no more reason to live.*

Late one night Cynthia Ann, exhausted, drifted into a restless doze. She awoke with a start. The small body next to hers lay still, at peace.

Cynthia Ann's wail pierced the gloomy silence of the cabin. In an instant, Orlena and Ruff were beside her. "Dead," she said, feeling as though her chest might explode with the pain.

Of course they would not listen to her, how it should be done. They refused her pleas to let her prepare the body properly, in the way of the People: her little knees tucked up against her chest, her eyes sealed with clay, and the body then wrapped in a blanket. Instead they dressed Prairie Flower in one of her new dresses, made from one of Amelia Cates's silk taffeta gowns, and laid her small body in a wooden box. Mr. and Mrs. Cates drove Cynthia Ann and the box with the body of Prairie Flower to a small cemetery near Ben Wheeler. Orlena and Ruff O'Quinn followed in their wagon. Silas met them there; one of Ruff's slaves had ridden over to tell them what had happened, and Silas came alone. He approached Cynthia Ann apologetically.

"Mary sends her sympathy," he said gruffly. "But she couldn't come. She's not been well since the baby was born, I'm sorry to say."

Cynthia Ann turned away.

They should have taken the wooden box to a cave or a natural crevice among the rocks and left it there. Instead, they dug a hole in the ground, lowered the box into the hole, and shoveled dirt on top of it. And they insisted that the preacher had to come along and read from that Bible and say all those things over the small, wasted body that meant nothing. Nothing at all.

CHAPTER TWENTY-NINE

From Lucy's journal, May 7, 1864

Why is it that every good thing that happens always comes mixed with something bad?

Papa returned from the war last week, so thin his tattered uniform hung on him like a rag on a stick. We are all very happy to have him home again in one piece, but I did not recognize him at first; the war has aged him so. He was accompanied by a man from Van Zandt County who served with him, Mr. George Shipley. Mr. Shipley is a friend of Orlena O'Quinn, Cynthia Ann's sister, and he brought with him tragic news: Prairie Flower is dead.

At first I could not stop crying, although Mama and Grandfather and the others try to comfort me, saying it is God's will and all for the best. This may be true, but I know that Cynthia Ann must be inconsolable. We all felt so sad, even Mama, who has not wasted any affection on Prairie Flower or her mother.

According to Mr. Shipley, Cynthia Ann was better off with Orlena and Ruff than she had been with Mary and Silas, and Prairie Flower was loved by all. But last fall Prairie Flower took sick, and despite the efforts of everyone, she died in December.

When he saw how I grieved, Mr. Shipley took the time to talk to me and to give me details that he had learned from his sister. It seems his sister is the same Mrs. Cates that Orlena mentioned in her letter. Mr. and Mrs. Cates had become quite attached to Prairie Flower and they were as saddened by the child's death as they might have been by the death of one of their own.

"How is Cynthia Ann?" I asked. "Has she accepted this cruel blow?"

He shook his head. "It was as though she had lost her senses," he said. "My sister said she wailed and keened until they couldn't stand to hear it anymore. She smeared her face with soot from the chimney and hacked off her hair. She cut her arms until they bled so much that she fainted. Orlena hid the knives and scissors, but that did not stop her from using sharp stones. It went on for days like that, they said, and then for weeks. She wouldn't speak the child's name. She couldn't bear to be anyplace that the child had been. She burned the toys Prairie Flower loved to play with, even the ragged little doll you made for her, Lucy."

I could hardly speak. "Where is she now?" I whispered.

"Ruff O'Quinn finally suggested that she go to stay at a sawmill he owns about twenty-five miles from his farm. There's a little cabin on the property, and nobody around to bother

her. They thought it would give her time to get over this."

"And she's there now? All alone?"

Mr. Shipley nodded. "Once a week Mr. Cates or Mr. O'Quinn goes down to visit her and make sure she has what she needs. I don't think there's anything more anyone can do."

When I trusted myself to speak, I told Mr. Shipley about my conversations with Cynthia Ann, and how I had helped her find our language again and even to learn to read and write a few words. Then I confided to him my "promiss" that she would someday be reunited with her son Quanah.

He smiled at me, a kindly smile. "That was quite a promise," he said. "You make promises that are hard to keep. Quanah is a dangerous fellow. They say he's joined the Quahadas, probably the fiercest of the Comanche bands."

"But she was his mother," I insisted. "He would never have harmed her!"

"It's not his mother I was thinking about," Mr. Shipley replied.

Mr. Shipley remained here for several days, but yesterday he left to return to his family in Ben Wheeler. (He is a widower whose wife died while he was serving with the cavalry, and his children are staying with his brother and sister-in-law.) He made it a point to speak to me privately before he left.

"You were a good friend to her when she needed a friend, Lucy. Maybe her only friend, the only one to listen to her. Life often takes away from us the thing we love best, and if we're lucky, we get something to take its place. I think your grandfather and everyone else meant well by bringing Cynthia Ann and Prairie Flower here. But they weren't meant to be among us. We—I mean all of us white people—took away her life as a Comanche, but what we had to offer her instead was not what she wanted. Or maybe she just didn't know *how* to want it. But you understood, Lucy."

I thanked George Shipley for that. It was helpful to me, and I was frankly sorry to see him go, although he has invited me to come to visit Mr. and Mrs. Cates to learn more about Prairie Flower's last days and to visit Cynthia Ann. Perhaps she will talk to me, and I can reassure her that I have not forgotten my "promiss."

I told him that I would, as soon as it becomes easier to travel. Promises get harder and harder to keep as we struggle here simply to survive this dreadful war. We seem in no great danger from the Blue Coats, but raids from the north by the Indians are increasing and shortages are worsening.

The worst privation, from my point of view, is that we have no paper. This little journal is nearly filled, although I have been taking care that every page has been used to the utmost, and as it is impossible for me to obtain another. The fate of the Parker family will no longer be recorded by me.

CHAPTER THIRTY

Ben Wheeler, Van Zandt Co., Texas, July 12, 1864

Dear Lucy,

I am sorry that circumstances have prevented your visit here, for now I must write the sad news that your cousin, Cynthia Ann Parker, passed from this earth Saturday a week ago. Our neighbors Joe and Bob Pagitt made her a decent coffin, and Mrs. Pagitt, who was so fond of little Tecks Ann, saw that she was decently prepared for burial. I went with them to the Foster Cemetery, some distance to the south of here, and we laid her to rest. The doctor says it was "la grippe," others say she starved herself to death. It is my belief that she died of a broken heart. A pity you never got to see her, for I am certain a visit of yours would have helped her. I am told she spoke kindly of you.

Forgive this poor writing paper, it was all I had. Conditions are no better here than in the past, and we can only pray for the end. My warmest regards to your family. I hope that your father is once again enjoying civilian life.

Yours sincerely,
George Shipley

CHAPTER THIRTY-ONE

Weatherford, Parker Co., Texas, April 21, 1883

> elping to go through the effects
> of my late grandfather, Isaac
D. Parker, who died one week ago today at the age of ninety,
I found the journal to which this note is hereby attached. It
is the journal I kept during my girlhood, in a book given to
me on my twelfth birthday, June 8, 1860, until the pages were
filled the summer of 1864. During those difficult years of the
War between the States, this journal was at times my only
friend and confidante, and as I reread those pages I am once
again moved to tears at the hardships we endured. We being
my grandfather, my parents, my brothers and sisters, and most
especially my cousin, Cynthia Ann Parker, whose life is chron-
icled in those pages.

I gave up my journal late in May of 1864, when shortages
of nearly everything plagued our lives and I had not one scrap

of paper left to write upon. This was before I learned that Cynthia Ann had died—of a broken heart, most assuredly— at the age of thirty-seven, only a few months after her little Prairie Flower had been taken from her, a sweet child of four or five years.

It was a disappointment to me that I was not able to keep my pledge to her—my "promiss"—that she would one day be united with her son Quanah. Our excuse was always that the war prevented it, but the truth is, I do not know how I would have brought about that meeting. Many stories about Quanah reached us, but it was impossible to separate fact from rumor. We did learn that he had apparently left his father's tribe, the Noconis, and thrown his lot in with the Quahadas, reputedly the most wild and hostile of all the Comanche tribes. And he earned some reputation as a ruthless leader who swept down repeatedly on defenseless frontier settlements. But we also heard that he never allowed his braves to kill the white women and children, out of fear that he might be killing his own mother and sister.

A dozen years ago, Quanah was a notorious war chief. But in the summer of 1874, his fortunes began to change. He attacked white buffalo hunters at the Battle of Adobe Walls and found himself defeated by superior forces. That was the last of the Comanche raids. A few months later, Col. Ranald Mackenzie attacked a Comanche camp in Palo Duro Canyon, and although most of the women and children escaped up the canyon walls and only a few braves died in battle, all of the Indians' belongings were destroyed. Most important, Col. Mackenzie ordered their horses killed, over a thousand of them. Without horses the Comanches were powerless. The survivors of that attack surrendered at Fort Sill, in Indian Territory, and went meekly to live on reservations.

But Quanah held out, and it was not until a year later that he agreed to surrender. The buffalo were disappearing, more soldiers were coming into the area every day, and Quanah must have realized that the old Comanche way of life was over.

I was married and had been living in Ben Wheeler with my husband and children for a dozen years when Quanah, who took his mother's name on the reservation and thereafter became known as Quanah Parker, began to search for his mother. Unfortunately, I knew nothing about this at the time, or I would have tried to contact him to tell him what I know.

Yesterday, among Grandfather's private papers, I found a letter that Quanah Parker had written to Grandfather in 1877, inquiring about Cynthia Ann Parker. It was a curious letter; I think he had written it himself, perhaps with some help from someone better acquainted with English. If such a letter ever reached the Parkers in our part of Texas, I heard nothing of it. Her brother Silas would not have said a word, because of Mary. And although I have cordial relations with Orlena and Ruff O'Quinn, I believe they may not have wished to have dealings with a man they consider a savage. Perhaps Grandfather made the same decision.

Certainly there was a new chapter for Grandfather in other areas of his life. In 1872, when he was a vigorous seventy-nine years old, Grandfather left our home in Birdville, turning it over to my father and Ben. He bought another tract of land near Weatherford, in what is now Parker County—named for him—and built a new double log house there, much like our old one. He even took some of the lilac bushes from around the cabin and planted them at his new home.

And then, to everyone's surprise, he remarried—a handsome young widow, Sallie Gaines, with four children of her own. In short order, he fathered three more children. The youngest, whom he named Abraham, was born on Grandfather's eighty-fourth birthday. Old Isaac lived an apparently happy and productive life until two weeks ago when he fell ill with a fever and died April 14, at the age of ninety.

The rest of us have gone on with our lives as best we can, despite many times of sadness as well as times of joy and hope. For a time after he came home from the war, we worried about Papa's health, but he did recover his strength, and soon the farm was producing again, with help from Jedediah and my brother Ben. Ben never did get around to marrying, although I know the Bigelows' daughter had taken quite a fancy to him. Martha and Jedediah had twin boys and two lively daughters. My brother James helps with the farm and has moved his family into the cabin with Mama and Papa ever since Grandfather built his Weatherford home. Sarah taught school until she married Mr. Edward Liggett.

Mama is still alive but very frail. She has never been the same since Daniel died in infancy.

My own life has been well blessed. I married George Shipley in November 1864, when I was sixteen years old. George was twenty-eight and already had children, and I found myself raising two rambunctious sons before my own babies started to come. The war had affected him deeply. He declined to work in Mr. Cates's salt mine and became a circuit-riding preacher. Such a life is at times quite taxing for all of us.

There are many times at the end of the day, when I am sitting on my porch with a dish of peas in my lap to shell or mending to be done, and I remember Cynthia Ann. She was thirty-four when she came to us, nearly my present age, and perhaps only now can I truly understand how she must have felt, pulled away from her family and friends, forced to live among such utterly strange people as we surely seemed to her. Already she and her little Prairie Flower have become legends, and her son Quanah may well take his place in history, too.

Signed,
Lucy Parker Shipley

CHAPTER THIRTY-TWO

Note from the author, Denton, Texas, January 1992

W hen history becomes legend, the facts are often lost, changed, or confused. This is what happened in the case of Cynthia Ann Parker, who was captured by Comanches at Parker's Fort, Texas, on May 19, 1836, and recaptured by Texas Rangers and U.S. cavalry troops near the Pease River on December 18, 1860.

Besides those important dates, historians are sure of only a handful of details regarding Cynthia Ann's life: They know that she had an Indian husband, Peta Nocona, and three children, one of whom, Quanah, was to become a great leader of the Comanches. They also know that after her recapture, Cynthia Ann and her daughter, Topsannah, lived for a time with her uncle, Isaac D. Parker, in Tarrant County, and were taken to Austin to visit the Texas State Legislature in the spring of

1861. They are sure that she later went to live with a brother, Silas, and after that a sister, Orlena. It is historically true that Isaac Parker for whom Parker County was named died on April 14, 1883 at the age of 90.

Beyond these and a few other meager facts, we are left with contradictions or total blanks.

Most sources state with reasonable certainty that Topsannah died December 15, 1863. But there are a few other sources that suggest that she was taken from Cynthia Ann. One man even came forward years later claiming to be Topsannah's son.

Furthermore, no one is sure exactly when Cynthia Ann Parker died. Some writers claim she died in 1864; one historian has found census records proving that she was still alive in 1870. At least three other dates have been stated without proof.

No one knows what her experiences were during her nearly twenty-five years with the Comanches. Some writers claim the People named her Naduah; others say she was called Preloch. It's not known when her famous son, Chief Quanah Parker, was actually born; estimates run from the early 1840s to more than a decade later. He might have been a teenager, a young brave, when his mother was captured at Pease River, or he might still have been a young boy at the time.

Was his father, Peta Nocona, killed at Pease River, as Sul Ross claimed? Or was he somewhere else that fateful day, as others have written? There are as many versions of the Pease River Massacre as there are writers to record them.

This jumble of facts and contradictions presents a challenge for the storyteller. I have taken the key facts of the history of Cynthia Ann Parker and used them as a framework on which to fashion the story of her life, as it could have been. Lucy

Parker, her brothers and sisters, and her journal are my fictional inventions. This fictional Lucy, however, would have been pleased to know that after Quanah Parker's death in 1911, Cynthia Ann and Prairie Flower were eventually buried by his side in Fort Sill, Oklahoma.

Carolyn Meyer

Bibliography

Useful Sources

DeShields, James T. *Cynthia Ann Parker: The Story of Her Capture*. Reprint. Dallas, TX: Chama Press, 1991.

Fehrenbach, T. R. *Comanches: The Destruction of a People*. New York: Alfred A. Knopf, 1974.

Gonzalez, Catherine Troxell. *Cynthia Ann Parker: Indian Captive*. Stories for Young Americans Series. Austin, TX: Panda Books, Eakin Press, 1980.

Hacker, Margaret Schmidt. *Cynthia Ann Parker: The Life and Legend*. Southwestern Studies, No. 92. El Paso, TX: Texas Western Press, The University of Texas at El Paso, 1990.

Holman, David. *Buckskin and Homespun: Frontier Clothing in Texas, 1820–1870*. Austin, TX: Wind River Press, 1979.

Matthews, Sallie Reynolds. *Interwoven: A Pioneer Chronicle*. 1936. Reprint. College Station, TX: A & M University Press, 1982.

Noyes, Stanley, *Los Comanches: The Horse People, 1751–1845.* Albuquerque: University of New Mexico Press, to be published 1993.

Wallace, Ernest and E. Adamson Hoebel. *The Comanches: Lord of the South Plains.* 1952. Reprint. Civilization of the American Indian Series, No. 34. Norman, OK: University of Oklahoma Press, 1987.

GREAT
EPISODES

Other titles now available:

TIMMY O'DOWD AND THE BIG DITCH
by Len Hilts

JENNY OF THE TETONS
by Kristiana Gregory

THE RIDDLE OF PENNCROFT FARM
by Dorothea Jensen

THE LEGEND OF JIMMY SPOON
by Kristiana Gregory

GUNS FOR GENERAL WASHINGTON
by Seymour Reit

UNDERGROUND MAN
by Milton Meltzer

A RIDE INTO MORNING:
The Story of Tempe Wick
by Ann Rinaldi

EARTHQUAKE AT DAWN
by Kristiana Gregory

THE PRIMROSE WAY
by Jackie French Koller

A BREAK WITH CHARITY
*A Story About the
Salem Witch Trails*
by Ann Rinaldi

*Look for exciting new titles to come in the
Great Episodes series of historical fiction.*